Calamity at the Circus

To Mike and Mary Means,
and Chris and Maggie,
with gratitude for your friendship and support.

Calamity at the Circus

JERRY JERMAN

VICTOR BOOKS

A DIVISION OF SCRIPTURE PRESS PUBLICATIONS INC.
USA CANADA ENGLAND

THE JOURNEYS OF JESSIE LAND

The Long Way Home
My Father the Horse Thief
Calamity at the Circus

Phantom of the Pueblo
Danger at Outlaw Creek

The Secret of Whispering Woods (Oct. '96)

Cover design by Scott Rattray
Cover illustration by Michael Garland
Copyediting by Afton Rorvik, Liz Duckworth

This is a work of fiction. Any resemblance to actual events
or persons, living or dead, is entirely coincidental.

Library of Congress Cataloging-in-Publication Data

Jerman, Jerry, 1949–
  Calamity at the circus / by Jerry Jerman.
    p. cm.—(The Journeys of Jessie Land)
  Summary: When nine-year-old Walter creates trouble at the circus for
himself, Jessie, and Leo, the kids become involved with tiger thieves and
other adventures.
  ISBN: 1-56476-551-2
  [1. Circus—Fiction. 2. Adventure and adventurers—Fiction.]
I. Title. II. Series: Jerman, Jerry, 1949–   Journeys of Jessie Land.
PZ7.J54Cal 1996
[Fic]—dc20
                                          95-52429
                                           CIP
                                           AC

1 2 3 4 5 6 7 8 9 10 Printing/Year 00 99 98 97 96

For information write Victor Books,
1825 College Avenue, Wheaton, Illinois 60187.

Chapter 1

"WALTER!" I screamed as my obnoxious cousin aimed his slingshot at the enormous gas balloon. I was so mad I could spit.

I leaped off my homemade bicycle and tore across the dusty field after Walter Scott Tyler. The hot California sun burned that June morning, but not nearly as fierce as my anger. I wanted to throttle that blond-headed kin of mine good.

I stopped just inches from Walter. He turned his pale face to stare up at me with his cool blue eyes. Dozens of brown freckles dotted his cheeks and nose. His clothes looked decent—clean white shirt and brown pants. Even almost new shoes. To see him, you might take him for a sweet, innocent child. But I knew better. Walter was no more sweet and innocent than a rattlesnake!

I grabbed his arm and gave the boy a good shake. He just smirked. Like he thought he'd won. But he hadn't. Not yet leastwise. Behind Walter the red and blue gas balloon swayed in the faint breeze. I'd never in my twelve years seen such a thing before. On it a mess of bold letters read:

COL. JACK'S
COLOSSAL CIRCUS
AND
DEATH-DEFYING
THRILL EXTRAVAGANZA!

The circus! Even though the arrival of my nine-year-old cousin and my uncle had just about ruined my life, at least I could still look forward to the circus.

Ripping the slingshot from Walter's grasp, I said to him, "Would you just stop being such a pest?"

He stuck out his bottom lip and nagged, "Phoo, Jessie Land. You think you're so great. Just 'cause your pop's got a job with Will Rogers and you gotta new house. And you got yourself a bike, though it's pretty ugly, an' a dumb ol' armadillo for a pet. SO WHAT?"

I refused to answer him, though every word he spoke was true enough. Except me thinking I was great, of course.

I gazed up to heaven and asked silently, *Why, Lord, did You have to bring him back into my life? I just have to know.*

Something snagged my arm. I spun around to see my friend Leo Little Wolf flinch. His pudgy brown hands flew up to cover his round face. He yelled, "Don't hit me, gal!"

"What on earth are you talking about?"

"That look on your face," he said, stepping back. "It plumb scart me."

I stood a head taller than him, though we were both the same age. He wore an orange cowboy shirt so bright it hurt my eyes to look at it. He scratched his wild black hair and chomped furiously on a big wad of gum. His dark eyes studied me. "You look jest like an angry hornet."

"I'm fit to be tied is what I am," I told him in a huff. I glanced around to look at Walter. He'd already taken off in the direction of the big tent the circus folks had put up. "Why'd he and Uncle Rudy have to come here now? Just when we get back from Arizona and have us a new house? *Why?*"

Leo shrugged and moved away. Untying his rope from the leather thong on his belt, he fashioned a lasso and commenced practicing amazing rope tricks. He lived with me and Mama and Daddy and seemed a kind of "almost-brother," but he wasn't blood kin. Not like Walter and his father, Uncle Rudy.

"I'll bet Uncle Rudy's still asleep in my bed," I complained. "How on earth does he expect to find a job lounging the day away?"

Leo said, "Don't know, gal. Maybe he plans to live off the fat of the Lands." He chuckled. The idea didn't strike me as funny. I groaned instead.

I thought of my plump, balding uncle sprawled across *my* bed. In *my* room. Snoring to beat the band. And here it was the middle of the morning. Well past time for a grown man to be up and out looking for work. He'd said it himself, just yesterday afternoon when he and Walter stepped off the train. He needed to find a job. Seemed the bank had threatened to foreclose on his and Aunt Edna's tiny gas station in Kansas. Sure enough, hard times hit everyone in 1935. But did that mean we had to take in Walter and Uncle Rudy? That I had to sleep on the couch in the living room instead of in my own new bed?

"We'd best catch up with that cousin o' yours," Leo remarked, coiling the rope and nodding toward the big top*, " 'fore he gits hisself into another fix."

My friend pushed off with his bike, a bright red beauty Will Rogers had given me after we rescued his stolen horse. I'd given the new bike to Leo and kept the one Daddy had fashioned from spare parts. Mine wasn't much to look at, especially with one not-quite-round wooden wheel, but it worked OK.

"Yeah," I agreed, climbing back on my bicycle. Walter had already gotten into plenty of fixes that morning. Like breaking my penny jar, which didn't have but nine pennies in it. Then he'd tried to pretend he wasn't flat out stealing from me. And like tying a string of tin cans to my pet armadillo's tail. Victoria probably would never come out from under the porch. Leastwise not so long as Walter lived with us.

Pedaling after Leo, I thought back. Just two days ago Leo and I'd returned from a trip to Arizona. We'd gone bike riding east of town and happened upon an abandoned house with blistered white paint. Stuck crooked on the clapboards, a colorful poster with a tiger and a clown's face announced the circus coming to Santa Monica in just a few days. We'd been so excited we rode all the way back to town to tell Mama and Daddy. That was when

---

*A glossary of circus slang appears at the back of the book.

Mama showed me the letter from Aunt Edna. Uncle Rudy and Walter would arrive soon. If Uncle Rudy found work, he'd send for Aunt Edna and their other children.

The thought of the entire Tyler clan descending on us made me shudder. I'd lived with my aunt and uncle in Liberal, Kansas, for a time while Mama and Daddy looked for work in California. The longest six months of my life. Seemed I could never do enough to please my aunt. Just about every day I got spanked, mostly for minding my own business or for Walter's pranks. While I'd forgiven my aunt, I didn't want her or any of those Tylers living near us, much less with us.

Please, Lord, make them stay in Kansas, I thought as I pedaled my old bicycle toward the big top.

Plenty of folks, mainly shirtless, brawny men, worked on the lot about us. Some hammered pegs, preparing to hoist a couple of small tents. One led a team of horses into a makeshift corral. Two set about scrubbing a great gray elephant. A man made up like a clown shook his finger in the face of a woman in blue jeans and black muddy boots. When I reached the big top, I hopped down, laid my bike in the grass, and chased after Leo. Walter wasn't anywhere in sight.

I caught up with my friend in front of a rickety-looking ticket booth. All of a sudden his shoulders slumped and he twisted around to face me.

"So much for the circus, gal," he sighed.

I peered over his head and saw the sign that had upset him so.

Admission 15¢

"Oh," I moaned. My nine pennies wouldn't even buy
one of us a ticket. Two weeks ago, Will Rogers had given
my parents one thousand dollars cash money as a reward
for finding his stolen horse. They spent every cent getting us a new house to live in and a few things to go
inside.

Still, maybe Mama and Daddy could spare forty-five
cents. After all, hadn't Mama told Leo and me to entertain
cousin Walter? Admission to the circus would be a small
price to keep the little troublemaker out of the house.

I started to tell Leo this, but before I could, his eyes
widened and he darted past me.

"Hey!" I snapped.

He stopped, frowned, and scratched his head.

"Naw, couldn't be," he muttered.

"Leo, what's got into you?"

He just shook his head. "Nothin', gal. Jest thought I
saw someone I know is all."

"Listen, we'd better find Walter before he causes an
elephant stampede or something," I said.

"You're right 'bout that," he agreed, taking one last
look past me.

We rounded the big top. Back here came the strong,
ripe odor of animals. Something like I used to smell on
our farm back in Oklahoma. We discovered Walter standing on the other side of a large cage made of iron bars.
Two lions lounged inside, yawning and eying the boy

without much curiosity. Their lazy manner put me in mind of Uncle Rudy. Yet despite their behavior, I panicked. My cousin was reaching his hands toward the bars, like he intended to touch the large beasts. I raced around the cage to him.

"Walter, get away from that cage!" I commanded, grabbing his arm. "Those're dangerous animals."

He turned and smirked. "Phoo. They're nothin' but a couple of big pussycats."

I ignored him and pulled him back. I kept backing us up. Walter struggled against me every step of the way.

"Gal," Leo called out. "Look out where—"

I backed us up until I bumped into something behind me. Walter glanced back and his eyes grew wide. What—?

Twisting around, I found myself staring into another cage. There, pressed right up against the bars and only inches from me, leaned an enormous tiger with glowing, yellow eyes and big, sharp teeth.

The creature roared and my arms and legs became suddenly useless. I froze.

Chapter 2

I stood still, every muscle tight, like a clenched fist. I didn't even breathe.

The tiger's orange, black, and white-striped face kept still too. Its fiery yellow eyes seemed to look right through me. I heard a rattly sound, like a cat purring, but much louder and deeper. I thought, *This is just a big kitty cat, Jessie Land. Look at those cute whiskers and furry orange ears.* But then the tiger opened its mouth, cocked its head, and let go another roar. I spied those sharp teeth, big as my fingers. This was no house pet.

My eyes swept up to the top of the cage. I saw a sign that read, simply, *Attila.* "N-n-nice Attila," I stuttered. "G-g-g-good boy." I felt my legs start to wobble. I think I would've collapsed in a heap if I hadn't felt a hand grab ahold of my arm and jerk me back.

"Gal, git yourself away from that critter 'fore he turns you into vittles," came Leo's voice.

Standing farther back from the cage with Leo and Walter, I bent over, trying to take deep breaths.

"Jessie Land, you big scaredy cat," teased Walter.

"Never you mind," I told my cousin. "You just stay with us and don't run off again."

My cross voice didn't impress him much. He walked around the tiger's cage, keeping his distance. Leo and I followed. Attila had taken to pacing back and forth. All the while the tiger stared at me with his fierce yellow eyes. Just seeing them made me think a fiery rage burned in the critter. I felt a chill rush through me. I had no intention of going anywhere near that animal's cage again.

Just then Leo grabbed my arm and pulled me along. "Lookit that, gal," he said, pointing to a shady spot ahead.

Under a tree stood a man dressed all in white, except for a pair of long, polished brown boots. But it wasn't his clothes that made me stare. It was his peculiar behavior. He posed in front of a tall mirror propped against the tree. He clutched a pistol in his right hand and a whip in his left. Every few seconds he'd point the pistol and give it a shake like he was shooting it. Then he'd crack the whip. I could hear him yelling something too but couldn't quite make out the words.

"What's that fella doin', gal?" Leo asked. For the first time that morning he stopped chomping his gum.

"I'm not sure, Leo," I admitted.

Even Walter seemed amazed at the man in front of us. The three of us watched as the man made his whip crack in the warm summer air. Then he aimed the pistol at his image in the mirror as if trying to shoot his own reflection.

He kept cracking the whip and aiming the pistol over and over. Like he was practicing. Then, abruptly, he swung around and stared at us.

Leo and Walter and I stared back.

At first the man looked irritated, like he didn't much care to be caught acting so odd. But quickly his mouth formed a smile. He waved us over with his whip hand.

"I see you, kiddos," he shouted. "Come over here."

I felt embarrassed to be caught staring. Still, I edged closer. Leo and Walter followed behind me.

The man stood only a few inches taller than me. He was darkly tanned and muscular. A handsome man with jet black hair, not a lick of it out of place. His smile faded as he studied us with his gray eyes. He seemed to be making up his mind about us. Then again he flashed a grin of bright white teeth. They seemed all the whiter against that dark face.

"You kiddos planning to come to this broken-down circus if it ever opens?" he asked, still grinning.

I didn't know what he meant by "if it ever opens," but I said, "We'd like to, sir. Though we don't really have enough mo—"

"Well, you be sure and catch my act," he said.

"Your act?" Walter said.

The man's grin widened. "I'm the Great Buchanan," he announced, bowing slightly. "Rand Buchanan. Facing death daily as the tamer of wild and ferocious animals."

"Whatcha doing in front of that mirror?" Walter asked.

"Er—just practicing my stance," the Great Buchanan replied. "When I'm in the cage with these beasts, I must always look confident and fearless. I've got to look just right." He turned around and peered at his reflection in the mirror as if checking to see that he still looked just right. "Here, I'll show you."

He reached out, grabbed my hand, and pulled me to the mirror. "Just stand there and look at yourself."

I did. I saw a girl of twelve with short red hair, brown eyes, and a determined chin that resembled her father's. I saw a pair of patched and faded overalls, a frayed white shirt, and shoes that had been plenty scuffed. I saw a girl who looked plumb embarrassed to be standing in front of a mirror just then. I felt my face heat up and saw it turning red as I gazed at my image.

"You're a pretty girl," the Great Buchanan said. "But when you face the big cats, you don't want pretty. You want fearless."

He handed me his pistol and whip. "Now you try it."

Clutching the gun in one hand and the whip in the other, I made a half-hearted attempt to imitate him. Mostly, though, I just looked embarrassed.

"Here, *lemme!*" Walter shrieked. "Lemme!" My cousin ripped the whip and gun from my hands.

"Walter! Careful with that gun," I warned.

"Don't worry, I never load it with real ammunition," the animal trainer said. "I use only blanks. For effect."

Walter tried to stand taller before the mirror. He pointed the whip and tried to crack the gun.

The Great Buchanan laughed. "Takes practice, kiddo."

"Don't you ever git scart in the cage with all them wild animals?" Leo asked.

The man's grin faded. "It's serious business. Every day I face death square in the face. Fear could kill me."

Fear would save me, I figured. I'd never get in the cage in the first place.

The Great Buchanan took back his whip and gun. A good thing. Even an unloaded gun in Walter's grip put me on edge.

Flashing us another bright smile, the animal trainer said, "I want you kiddos to cheer for me, you hear? If this sorry old circus ever gets off the ground that is."

"What do you mean?" I asked him.

He glanced about, then leaned near and said in a low voice, "If I were a betting man, I'd say this circus is on its last legs. Cami just can't handle it like the old colonel did. But the Miller Brothers Circus will be buying her out soon. Then my career will really take off."

"Miller Brothers?" Leo asked, swinging his lasso into the air and twirling it about.

"A fine old circus. And they've already spelled out that I'll be getting top billing. I would be their headline act."

"Gee, that's swell," Leo admitted.

The Great Buchanan turned back toward the mirror. He squinted at his reflection and grinned. "Excuse me, kiddos. I've got to practice. I've got to be in top form."

"We have to be getting along ourselves," I admitted. "Hope we get to see your act, sir."

"Don't forget," the animal trainer said, his pistol pointed in the air. "The Great Buchanan."

I turned to nudge Walter along. But there wasn't anyone beside me to nudge. My cousin, Walter, the Great Troublemaker, had vanished. Again.

Chapter 3

My heart pounded as Leo and I raced around the big top searching for Walter. I just knew we'd find the boy up to no good. I wanted to grab Leo's rope and hogtie the little varmint so he'd never be able to wander off again. My anger made my heart pound even harder.

I dodged all sorts of circus folks, most of them strong-looking, sweaty men who carried boxes and heavy ropes and equipment about under the hot sun. I spotted a woman in what looked like a shimmering bathing suit. Perched atop a white horse, she rode about in a circle. Imagine! Then I saw the clown still arguing with the young woman in boots and jeans. The woman shot Leo and me an angry glance as we raced by. It made me feel like we didn't belong in this place.

But I had no choice. I had to find Walter. I'd promised Mama and Daddy to watch out for him, and a promise was a promise.

Where was that little troublemaker?

When I stopped to look around, Leo slammed into me. Ooof!

"Gal, gimme some warnin', will ya?" he cried, rubbing his head.

"Where'd he go, Leo?"

"Can't we jest forget about him since he don't seem to be nowhere about?" my friend asked.

"You don't know Walter," I said. "When he disappears, that's when he really gets into mischief."

The canvas flaps of the big top were spread wide, like an open door. Just the kind of place that would attract Walter. I nodded to Leo and we slipped inside.

"Wow, gal, this place's mighty big!" exclaimed Leo.

He was right. The tent rose high and stretched wider than any barn I'd ever seen. I saw a couple of men hauling in long wooden boards and setting them up for folks to sit on. Another man led a big, gray elephant around in a ring. When he cracked a whip, the elephant would rear up and walk on its back legs. Amazing! Sawdust had been spread over the ground, and here and there boxes sat piled up. No one inside paid Leo and me any mind.

It seemed magical, this place. Like nothing you'd find anywhere else in 1935. All of a sudden I couldn't wait till the circus opened. I wanted to sit in the stands and see it all. I smiled as my eyes traced the sides of the tent, then where it sloped up and up—climbing to a high, dark ceiling. Far above the ground I spied the trapeze and the tightrope stretched from pole to pole. Then I saw him! There on a platform, so high above the ground, perched Walter Scott Tyler.

Oh, no! Walter was usually such a coward. But every so often—like now!—he'd go and do something stupid . . . and dangerous.

"WALTER!" I shouted. In my mind flashed all sorts of disasters. Most of them ended with cousin Walter falling to certain injury on the sawdust-strewn floor.

"Gal, how're we gonna git him down?" Leo asked, scratching his head. "Or do we really want 'im down? Maybe—"

"Leo! Of course we've got to get him down. Before he . . . ." I stopped myself. I didn't want the disasters in my head to become any more real.

I stomped around the ring until I stood right under the boy. I looked up, cupped my hands around my mouth, and shouted, *"Walter, come down this instant!"*

He didn't move or look down. Didn't he hear? I called out again.

He stayed put, perched up there like some bird. I knew I had no choice. I'd have to go fetch him. I commenced climbing up the skinny ladder that led to the platform.

"Gal, whatcha doin'!" Leo cried.

"I've got to go after him," I grumbled as I stepped on up.

"But, gal . . . "

"Just stay there," I told him. "You may have to pick up the pieces."

As I climbed, I kept yelling up at Walter. "You come down from there real quick, Walter Scott Tyler. Or you'll be in a heap of trouble." But he paid me no mind.

The narrow ladder went straight up and so did I. After a bit my hands grew sweaty. The air seemed warmer. I began to feel dizzy and gripped the rungs tight. *"Don't look down, Jessie Land,"* I told myself over and over.

When I'd nearly reached the platform, I demanded, "Come down from there right now." My voice sounded weak and shaky.

This time Walter leaned back and looked at me. Without seeming the least bit scared, he threw me a mischievous grin. Then I saw in his hand something that terrified me.

His slingshot!

"Walter, don't you dare use that weapon in here," I threatened, my voice still quivering.

"Phoo, Jessie Land," he laughed. "Just you watch me now."

"No, Walter, don't!" I cried.

I climbed up two more steps. High enough to get my hands on the edge of the platform. Looking at my cousin, I saw his arms come up. He took aim with the dreaded slingshot. Before I could yell again, he fired.

I glanced down. My stomach flip-flopped at the sight of the ground. My head swimming, I clung tighter to the ladder. *Don't look down,* I reminded myself.

"Walter, put that slingshot back in your pocket and come down right now," I warned him. "Or I'll tell your father what you've been up to."

"Phoo, you just do that," he sneered as his arms came up. He took aim again.

"No, Walter, *don't!"* I shouted.

"Here goes nothin'," he sang out.

The elastic band snapped. I didn't look down. I didn't

need to. The sounds below told me everything.

The rock must've struck the elephant. I heard a loud grunt and a dull thud. Suddenly a blaring trumpet-like blast filled the air. The whole tent seemed to shake as the elephant charged forward. Then a cracking crash of lumber echoed up to me. I heard the wooden planks splinter and pictured the elephant's stomping feet. Angry shouts rose up. Still, I heard the elephant continue to stomp about.

Walter was giggling and pointing at the scene below. I reached up and yanked the slingshot from the boy's hand.

"Walter, you'll be punished for this," I growled at him through clenched teeth. My anger boiled inside me, making me forget my fear for the moment. "You—"

Then I heard something else. From below, a woman's voice. Glancing down, I caught sight of the woman I'd seen earlier, the one in jeans and muddy boots, who'd thrown us the angry look.

"Come-down-here-right-now!" she screamed at us through a red megaphone she held up to her mouth.

Now Walter'll get what he deserves, I thought.

Till, of course, I noticed my hand and saw that I was the one clutching the boy's slingshot.

Chapter 4

Walter and I eased down the ladder, with him going first. The young woman stood waiting for us as we stepped onto the sawdust-covered ground. I looked for Leo but didn't see him anywhere.

"Just what were you towners doing up there?" the woman demanded.

A red megaphone hung around her neck by a thin chain. Outside the big top I'd seen her arguing with a clown. He stood just behind her now staring at Walter and me with his large, painted eyes.

The woman brought up the megaphone and yelled through it, *"Hey, I'm waiting!"*

What outright rudeness! But I didn't want Walter lying, so quickly I explained, "Sorry, ma'am. I just went up there to get my cousin down."

"And you decided to take a shot at the bull while you were at it?" she asked, pointing her slender finger at the slingshot I held. Her large brown eyes stared at me.

Bull? I guessed that to be her word for elephant.

I looked at the tall, thin, young woman. Her long, dark brown hair spilled out under a crumpled gray hat that partly shaded her face. She wore a faded, blue work shirt and even more faded blue jeans. The legs of her jeans were stuffed into a pair of muddy black boots. Even in men's clothes, she had a pretty, delicate look to her. But her behavior wasn't delicate. I wondered who she could be.

"No, ma'am," I said. I wanted to say, "It was Walter! *He* did it." But I kept still. I didn't figure she'd believe me since I held the weapon.

"Well, your little prank caused plenty of damage," she told me. "See that bleacher over there? It's broken in three places. Now I've got to get someone who's already busy to fix it. And it'll cost me. You have any jack to pay for it?"

"Jack?"

She nodded, impatient with my ignorance. "Jack, kush, kale. You know, *money*."

I shook my head. "No ma'am."

"I didn't think so," she replied. "You little lot loafers never do."

Lot loafers? She sure used a lot of strange words. But I knew enough to understand she'd called us a name, and I didn't much care for it.

The woman turned and said to the clown, "Marty, get another hand and fix that bleacher. There's scrap lumber in the back of the green flatbed."

The clown sighed. "Look, Cami, it's like I been tellin' you. I'm sick and tired of your dumping every odd job you can find on me. 'Marty, fix the broken bleacher. Marty, replace the frayed ropes on the gas balloon. Marty, do

this, Marty do that.' I didn't hire on to do roustabout
work. I'm a joey, not a hand."

The woman turned to face him. "You never replaced
those frayed ropes. And it's still got to be done. We've
gone over this. You know I couldn't afford to keep all the
roustabouts on."

"I'll tell *you* something," the clown warned, his voice
angry. "You keep asking the other joeys to do odd jobs
and they'll *all* run out on you. Every last one of 'em."

For a moment they stood silent, looking eye to eye.
Neither one seemed ready to back down.

"Marty, in an outfit this size, everyone's got to pitch
in," the young woman said finally. Her voice sounded
tired but firm. "I've been a rubber man. I've worked on
the hammer gang. Why, before we left the last town,
Rand even came out here to hang paper."

Rubber man? Hammer gang? Hang paper? What did all
this mean?

"Maybe Rand should concentrate on his act instead,"
the clown sassed. "He didn't look too good last week."

"The point is, nobody has just one job," she fired back.

"No, the point is, we haven't been paid, Cami. Not in a
long time."

The young woman took a deep breath. I wondered if
she'd give up now or keep arguing with the man. She
replied, "We ought to have a good run here. I can pay you
when we finish this stand."

"We haven't had a good run since you took over as old
man of this circus," the clown protested. "Every box of-

fice has netted us nothing but horse feed. And it seems like every time we turn around some catastrophe happens."

He turned to walk away, then stopped. He wagged his finger at her. "I can do nothing and not get paid. The whole crew knows that Miller Brothers outfit made you an offer. No sense holding out. You oughta sell this dog and pony show and be done with it. But no, you're just like the old colonel. Too stubborn and too proud."

"Leave Father out of it," she threatened. "You hear me?"

"Yeah, I hear you," the clown answered. "Now you hear me. I quit. Miller Brothers made me an offer too. They offered me a *paying* job."

With that, the clown turned and tramped away, his floppy shoes stirring up little clouds of sawdust. I glanced at the woman. Her pretty mouth drooped and her eyes became shiny. I looked away, not wanting to watch if she commenced crying.

Instead, I heard her stomp out of the big top. I shoved Walter and we followed, at least as far as the entrance where Rand Buchanan now stood. Where was Leo?

Outside, I heard the young woman shout, "I'll never give up, Marty! You hear me? *Never! Never!*"

"Come on, kiddos," the Great Buchanan said quietly.

He led us out of the tent. We stopped when we saw the young woman, her fists clenched, just a few feet away. The clown was gone.

"Things haven't turned out well for Camilla Starr," the

animal trainer whispered. "Look at her. This circus is just too much for her. It's pushed her over the edge, I fear."

I didn't know what he meant. Then I watched as the young woman spun around and gazed up at a banner tied to the side of a nearby wagon. Her eyes tightened and a look of determination came over her face. My eyes drifted from her to the banner.

It showed a larger-than-life picture of a man wearing a bright red cape. He appeared broad as a barrel and waved a black cane in the air. His gray-streaked brown hair hung well down over his collar, and he sported a carefully trimmed gray beard. His dark eyes seemed to pierce right through a person. He looked like he could step out of that banner and come to life. Above his picture I read the words:

Col. Jack Starr
Companion of Teddy Roosevelt!
Hero at San Juan Hill!
Founder and owner of this acclaimed Circus!

The young woman kept staring at the image of the man. She muttered something. I couldn't hear all of her words, but she seemed to be making some sort of promise.

I glanced at the Great Buchanan. He stood watching the woman and shaking his head. "See what I mean?" he whispered. "The poor girl has gone loco."

"Who is she?" I asked.

"Cami Starr. Daughter of the late Col. Jack. That's him up there." He indicated the man pictured on the banner. "She took over the circus when the colonel died a few months back. But like I said, it's just too much for the likes of a twenty-two-year-old female."

Suddenly exploding around the corner of the big top came Leo.

"Where've you been?" I asked.

He seemed shaken, like he'd just seen something that spooked him. He shook his head and didn't speak.

The young woman turned, planted her hands on her hips, and scowled.

To the animal trainer she squawked, "You should be practicing, Rand. Especially with the stripe since he's been acting so edgy."

"I was just talking to these kiddos, Cami," the Great Buchanan replied, his teeth clenched. I figured he didn't like being told what to do. Especially by a woman, and one a good bit younger than himself to boot.

Cami Starr brought up the red megaphone. Through it she snapped, *"Well?* Leave them to me, you hear? *Go on!"*

Rand Buchanan slapped his hand against his holstered pistol and stalked off in the direction of the tiger's cage.

The circus owner tromped up to the three of us, her boots crunching on the dirt. I could almost picture her clutching a whip and taming a few wild beasts herself. Her eyes pierced right through me. I glanced back at the banner. She had her father's eyes all right.

"Well, how do you lot loafers plan to pay for the damages?" she asked.

"Damages?" muttered Leo.

"I'll tell you later," I said.

For a moment I just stood silent, looking at her. I could tell she didn't have much regard for us. But I didn't have much regard for being called names either. I decided to try to do something about it. First, I'd give her a chance to be civil. I took a deep breath and stepped up to the woman.

Sticking out my hand, I declared, "My name's Jessie Land, ma'am."

Cami Starr stared at my hand like it was covered with mud. Then her eyes went to my face. A curious look replaced her frown. Reluctantly, she reached out and took my hand.

"Cami Starr," she said.

I introduced Leo and Walter. She nodded at them.

"You children shouldn't've been in the big top," she said, her voice kinder now. "How're you going to pay for that broken bleacher?"

I thought quickly. "Well, ma'am, it looks like you might be shy on help. Maybe we could work off the damages, doing odd jobs and such."

Her frown softened. Nodding, she said, "Maybe you could at that. But don't get the idea you'll get into the circus for free or that you'll earn anything extra. You've got a big debt to repay. Besides, I'm sure you heard what the joey said. I can't pay my regular performers right now. I sure can't pay you."

"Don't you fret," I piped up. "We'll work hard. And we'll do a good job too."

Walter shuffled beside me. He grumbled, "Phoo, I ain't workin' for nothin'."

I grabbed him by the shoulders and looked hard at him. "Oh, yes you will. It was *your* slingshot, remember, that got us into this fix." I realized then that I still held the weapon. I reached out, grabbed his hand, and slapped the slingshot into his palm.

"Ow!" he whined, even though I hadn't hurt him any. If his mother'd been there, he would've gone running to her. He'd whine that I'd struck him with a stick or some such thing.

Marching away, Cami Starr called back to us, "You kids come along."

I sighed, relieved. At least we'd be able to work off the damages. I sure didn't want to report to Mama and Daddy that Walter had torn up the circus with his shenanigans.

Leo came up beside me and whispered, "Gal, what happened? And what exactly didja git us into?"

I told him what Walter had done under the big top. He looked none too happy at the prospect of working to pay off damages caused by my cousin.

I grabbed Walter's sleeve and jerked him along as Cami Starr led us behind the big top. She walked plenty fast, her dark brown hair swinging beneath her crumpled gray hat.

The smells of animals grew stronger as we threaded

our way around piles of boxes and equipment.

"*Phew!*—this place stinks!" Walter complained, holding his nose. "Let's get outta here."

City boy! I just held tighter to his arm and tugged him along after me.

He was right though. It did smell pretty bad. And the farther we went, the stronger the odor. It put me in mind of when I'd helped Daddy muck out a barn, back in Oklahoma. And when I helped some with the horses on Will Rogers' ranch. Secretly I hoped we wouldn't be cleaning up after the circus animals.

We passed another banner picturing Col. Jack. I caught up with Cami Starr and said, "Col. Jack was your father?"

She stopped in her tracks. At first she stared straight ahead. Then she sighed, turned to me, and replied, "My father, yes. Founder, owner, and wild animal trainer."

"I'm sorry to hear he died, ma'am," I told her.

Her eyes fixed on me, piercing right through me again. I glanced away. "Yes, well, it's been six months now. I've been trying to hold this circus together ever since. Though I'm beginning to wonder why."

She sounded so sad I wanted to say something to take her mind off her circus troubles. I said the first thing that popped into my head. "I thought the Great Buchanan trained the wild animals."

She gave me a funny look. "The Gr—? Oh, yes. He took over Father's act."

"Did a wild critter eat your pop?" my cousin blurted out.

I felt my face heat up. Of all the rude remarks! I gave Walter a good hard jab.

He yanked away and screamed, "Owww! Stop it!"

"That's none of your business," I told him sternly. To Cami Starr I said, "Sorry, ma'am."

"I jest wondered," Walter whined, his lower lip stuck out.

"Well, if you must know he got careless one night," Cami Starr said.

"What happened?" asked Walter. I gave him a hard look, though I had to admit I was plenty curious myself.

"It was a stripe," she replied, her voice wavering.

"A stripe?" Walter asked.

Cami Starr looked away. I thought her eyes looked teary. "A tiger, boy. A tiger killed him."

Chapter 5

"You mean the tiger *ate* him?" Walter gasped.

I jabbed my elbow into the little rascal. How could he say such a thing to the man's own daughter?

Cami Starr, though, answered without batting an eye. "Stripes are dangerous. Sometimes even deadly."

"But how'd it happen?" Walter persisted.

That was the last straw. I'd heard enough of his rude questions. I stomped on the boy's foot.

"Yeeeowwwww!" Walter exclaimed as he commenced hopping about.

I said, "What Walter meant is what happened to the *tiger* after the—uh—accident?"

Cami Starr glanced over at the tiger cage and replied, "We destroyed him. Attila there is his brother."

I looked at the cage and saw the Great Buchanan poking a long wooden pole through the bars. Attila the tiger slapped at it with his enormous paws and bared his jagged, deadly teeth. I didn't like the looks of those teeth one whit. I recalled the Bible story of Daniel in the lions' den. It had to be a miracle that Daniel kept his wits and escaped alive. Mostly, though, I thought about Cami Starr losing her father that way. It was plain awful.

"Come on," the young circus owner commanded. "I've got work to do. And you do too."

Stepping over piles of rope thick as my arm, we wound around three or four large trucks with the words *Col. Jack's Colossal Circus* painted on the sides. We caught up to Cami Starr at a badly dented, dark green flatbed truck. She yanked open the door and leaned into the cab. In the distance I heard the cries of wild animals. If I'd closed my eyes I could've imagined myself in some jungle. *Jessie Land*, I thought, *you've come a long way from Oklahoma.*

When Cami Starr backed out of the cab, she held a bundle of circus posters in her arms. She handed them to me. I noticed they were just like the one I'd seen tacked on the abandoned house outside town.

Then Cami Starr climbed up onto the flatbed and fetched a burlap bag of tacks and a couple of hammers. She handed these to Leo and Walter.

She hopped down from the truck and brushed off her jeans. Then, hands on her hips, she directed, "Tack up this paper around town. And don't try to dump any of them either. 'Cause I'll find out. When you get through, come back and I'll have something else for you to do. That clear?"

I nodded. "Yes, ma'am."

For an instant I thought she might smile. But I was wrong. She just stared at us with those dark brown eyes of hers. Then she said, "OK, off with you. I want all that paper up this morning."

With that, she turned and stalked off. I wondered what

went on in the head of a young woman whose own father got himself killed by a tiger. And who now had charge of a circus where nothing seemed to be going right. Maybe that explained why she never cracked a smile.

No sooner had she walked away than Rand Buchanan came up. He wore a puzzled grin.

"You kiddos still here?" he asked. "I thought Cami would order you off the lot for breaking that bleacher."

"We're working off the damages," I confessed. "Tacking up posters in town."

His eyebrows shot up and he rubbed his dark chin. "Oh? And will that take care of the debt?"

"Well, not exactly," I said. "Once we finish, she'll have more work for us to do."

The Great Buchanan threw back his head and laughed. He looked in the direction Cami Starr had gone. "She's got her father's cheapskate blood all right," he said. "I don't think breaking that rotten bleacher put her out any."

"I knew she was askin' us to do too much work for that crummy little bench," Walter complained.

"You've got no room to talk," I told my cousin. *"You* got us into this fix in the first place."

"Don't be too hard on the kiddo," the animal trainer said. "He's right. I'll bet Miller Brothers Circus would at least pay you in cash if you worked for them."

"I wish *they* owned this fleabag circus," Walter grumbled.

I glanced at Leo who stood off a ways twirling his lasso.

He frowned as he stared off in another direction. What had gotten into that boy? He'd hardly said a word all day and seemed lost in his own world.

"All in good time, kiddo," the Great Buchanan said to Walter. "They'll own this outfit soon enough." He ran his hand over his perfect hair as if to straighten it. "Then I'll get my big break. Miller Brothers knows talent. I expect a top job. Star billing!" He closed his eyes and spread his hands apart. "The Great Buchanan!" he said, beaming.

All this talk about jobs gave me an idea. "Speaking of jobs," I piped up, "Walter's father's looking for work. Do you think Miller Brothers would give him a job too?"

The Great Buchanan nodded, grinning. His white teeth flashed. "They'll need plenty of good workers to make this dog and pony show a success. If he's a good hand, I'd say he has a chance. I could put in a good word for him myself."

My heart leaped at the news. *You did it, Jessie Land. You got Uncle Rudy a job! He and Walter can find their own place to stay. Now when Aunt Edna and those other Tyler kids move out here, we won't have to put them up.*

The animal trainer walked off with a wave of his whip. We set out with our load of posters, tacks, and hammers.

When we reached the spot where our bikes lay, Leo said, "Gal, do ya think a pa might miss his kid if they'd been away from each other for a spell? That he might even go lookin' for him?"

His question caught me by surprise. I didn't know what to say. I didn't want to think about it either because something had just popped into my head. Something about Uncle Rudy getting a job with the circus.

A circus doesn't stay in one place. It travels around. Uncle Rudy and Aunt Edna wouldn't even have to live in Santa Monica. They'd travel with the circus, wouldn't they?

Ignoring Leo, I said to my cousin, "Isn't this great, Walter? Your father might have a job real soon." I became excited just thinking about it.

Walter just groaned. "Phoo, my pop won't work for no stinky circus."

I paid him no mind. Surely in these hard times my uncle would take any job he got offered. I smiled to myself. Yes, of course he would. Soon I'd be rid of Uncle Rudy and Walter for good!

Chapter 6

As soon as we got to town, Walter leaped from Leo's handlebars. I suspect the boy figured he'd been good for a whole ten minutes, and he couldn't stand it any more. He raced across the street and strolled along a row of stores. I kept one eye on him as Leo and I began tacking up posters. My joy at finding Uncle Rudy a job quickly faded.

I said to Leo, "You know what makes me mad?"

"What, gal?"

"We could be doing this work for tickets to the circus. Instead, we've got to pay for that bleacher. It's all Walter's fault if we miss the circus."

My friend said, "What I wonder's how come your cousin got us into this fix and he ain't doin' a lick o' work?"

"Because he's Walter," I replied angrily. "Work and Walter just don't go together. He's the spitting image of his father."

I slapped a poster against a fencepost and hammered it up. Looking at the picture helped take my mind off Walter some. The poster made the circus look like a happy, colorful place. Where white-faced clowns made you laugh and women in shimmering costumes soared high over your head on the trapeze. Even the tiger didn't appear too menacing. Compared to the bright picture, Santa Monica seemed drab and dreary.

But Santa Monica was like everywhere else that summer. Folks stood in line for hours if they thought a job might be had. Idle men slumped on park benches in dusty clothes. When the soup kitchens opened, hungry folks with lined faces and dark, staring eyes appeared from nowhere. Government trucks loaded with apples or potatoes or bread brought swarms of men, women, and children into the streets, all hoping to get an armload of free food for their families. This was what life was like for folks without jobs.

Folks like Uncle Rudy. All at once I felt truly sorry for my unkind thoughts toward my Kansas kin.

But then I glanced across the street and saw Walter filch a handful of purple grapes from a produce stand. Before I could yell at him, the boy picked the fruit from the stems and commenced popping them into his mouth one after another. My sympathy for the Tyler clan vanished quick as the grapes.

"Walter!" I screamed at the little thief.

His head shot up. When he saw me, he pitched what fruit he hadn't eaten into an empty lot, hurried up the sidewalk, and turned down a side street.

"Leo, we've gotta corral Walter," I said, furious at my cousin. "If he gets into trouble, so do we."

"Well, let's tack up some posters, quick like, while we go," he suggested. "We won't never git 'em up otherwise."

We hustled up the street, tacking up posters as we went. We went so fast, I feared the posters would soon tear loose and end up lying in the dusty streets. I sure didn't want Cami Starr mad at us. But I didn't want Walter roaming loose either.

When we reached the side street I'd seen Walter turn down, the boy was nowhere about. He sure could cover a lot of ground for someone so inclined to be lazy.

At the next corner, still no sign of my cousin.

"Where'd he go?" I cried.

"Take it easy, gal," Leo said as he hammered a poster on a telephone pole. "He'll turn up."

"I know he'll turn up," I replied. "It's what he turns up doing that worries me."

We kept tacking up the posters, all the while on the lookout for Walter.

We came across a small boy crying as he gripped the handle of an overturned wagon. The contents—a heap of sand from the beach—lay spilled at the boy's dirty, bare feet. Walter!

On the next block we saw a grocer in a white apron picking up oranges that lay scattered across the sidewalk. Three flat orange blobs in the street showed where a car had come by. The man stood and faced us, clenching an orange in each hand. His red face and gritted teeth made me step back. I feared he might squeeze those oranges till they popped.

Walter'd been through here all right.

We had tacked up most of the posters when I finally

spotted Walter. He stood a block away on our side of the wide, busy street. I took a deep breath, all set to give the boy a piece of my mind.

Abruptly, Walter sprang into the street. He dodged one car, then stopped right smack in front of another. The driver slammed on his brakes and hammered his horn.

Aaaaaooooooooooooogggggggaaaaaa!

"Lookit 'im!" Leo exclaimed. "If he was a cat, he would've jest used up eight lives."

I ran to the curb. Cars kept coming. I couldn't cross.

"I can't wait to get my hands on him," I said, my fists clenched tight.

I watched as Walter went to the open door of a large metal building across the street. He glanced back at me, then slipped inside. The sign over the door read:

Jensen's Warehouse. We store anything.

What now?

An instant later he came out of the building dragging a large square board.

"What's he aimin' to do?" Leo wondered aloud as we stood on the curb and watched.

"I'm afraid to guess."

But I didn't need to guess. I saw with my own eyes as Walter propped up the board beside the open door. Then he raced around the side of the building. My mouth dropped open as I read the sign:

NOW HIRING

No! How could the boy do such a mean thing?

The "Now Hiring" sign worked like a fishhook and a fat worm in a good fishing hole. At first a few men standing about spotted it. They came running over and lined up at the door. Soon other men noticed the activity and came over too. Cars slammed on their brakes. One man stopped his car right in the middle of the street, leaped out, and ran to get in line. Horns blared. Then all the horns and ruckus attracted more folks.

"Oh, those poor folks," I moaned. "We've got to do something."

"I 'spect we'd best go fetch that sign," Leo replied.

It had taken only minutes for the swarm of hopeful people to gather outside the building. They would soon be very disappointed. All because of Walter's prank.

When the traffic eased up enough, Leo and I dropped our posters and hammers and raced across the street. We joined the throng of men and women huddled outside the building.

"Come on," I tugged at Leo's arm.

We elbowed our way through the crowd and made our way to the front.

Someone yelled, "Hey, you kids! Get in the back of the line!"

A deep voice boomed out, "Kids in line? Git 'em outta here! My family's half-starved."

I had to do something. Swallowing hard, I fought to get my courage up. Then I called out, "There's been a mistake. There're no jobs here. The sign—it's just a prank."

"What's she talkin' 'bout?" a voice rang out. "No jobs?"

Someone else cried, "Don't listen to 'er! The sign's up. I seen it myself."

A burly man in a tattered blue suit shoved Leo and me out of the way.

"Hey," Leo yelled.

"Please!" I shouted. "It's all a mistake."

"Git along, sister," the man warned.

I felt hands grabbing me, pushing me back, and pitching me out of the crowd. I skidded to a stop in the dust. Leo got shoved out right behind me. It was no use—these folks wouldn't listen. Leo and I edged away. Then I spotted him. Walter. He leaned out around the corner of the building watching the scene and laughing his fool head off.

I took off after him and grabbed him by his collar before he could escape. *"Got you!"* I declared.

"Lemme go," he cried, his laughter turning to a babyish whine. "I'll tell my pop."

"Go ahead," I said. "And I'll tell him everything you've been up to." I gave him a good shaking.

"Gal, ease up on 'im," Leo hollered.

"Don't worry," I said. "I won't kill him—not yet."

I dragged Walter back to the front of the warehouse. Some of the folks had stomped off. But some men were angry and yelling for the owner.

"Listen!" I called out to the folks in line. "This boy— he's got something to say." Walter had taken to cowering behind me, his hands clenching my overalls tight. I pulled him out and said, "Go on. Tell them what you did."

"I don't know whatcher talkin' about," Walter whined.

I heard a vehicle screech to a stop. I looked up and saw the sheriff getting out of his car. "Confess," I warned, "or Sheriff Colley'll likely take you off to jail."

Walter sank down to the ground and commenced bawling like a baby.

All at once a man in a dirty white shirt and a bow tie came out of the factory. "What's goin' on out here?"

Sheriff Colley, a tall, flabby man in a tight-fitting uniform, walked up. He couldn't speak at first, owing that he'd just stuffed a good-sized hunk of sandwich into his mouth. Mustard dripped across the front of his shirt. I'd had dealings with him before. He had once mistakenly thought my father was a horse thief.

"What's the trouble here?" he mumbled, still chewing.

The man in the bow tie frowned at the sheriff and snapped, "That's what I'd like to know."

"It's—it's all a prank," I stammered. "Tell them, Walter."

Walter glanced up at the two men and at the folks standing in line. He rubbed his eyes with his fists and slowly stood up. I figured he was plenty sorry for what he'd done and was ready to set things right.

Instead, he pointed at me and Leo. "It was them two," he lied. *"They* put up that sign and run off. I was gettin' ready to tell on 'em when she grabbed me."

My mouth dropped open. I looked at Leo and he looked at me, his dark eyes wide.

"Walter Scott Tyler!" I cried. To the sheriff I said, "He's

lying. We saw him put that sign up ourselves."

The man in the bow tie shook his head and told folks to move on. There weren't any jobs. I heard muttering and low curses as the people moved away. They gave me and Leo plenty of ugly looks too.

Sheriff Colley pulled me aside. I noticed a smear of mustard on his chin.

"You kids know what you did here?" he asked. "You done something awful. You gave these poor folks hope and then yanked it away from them. They don't appreciate it, and I don't neither." He wagged his finger at me. "Now I don't wanna catch the likes of you in trouble again. Or else."

The sheriff may've said "you kids," but he looked straight at me. I didn't know what he meant by "or else," but I didn't want to find out.

Chapter 7

When the sheriff's car pulled away, I grabbed my cousin's arm and pulled him after me.

"Walter, I've never been so embarrassed in all my born days," I shouted. "Don't you *ever* even think about doing something like that again."

Of course, warning Walter not to get into any more trouble was like warning a dog not to bark. Trouble just naturally followed him. And knowing that just made me angrier. When I finished ranting, the boy rubbed his eyes and made some fake sobbing noises. Then he took off.

"Walter, come back here!" I yelled.

But he'd already dashed across the street and dodged down an alley.

"I can't take much more of him," I complained to Leo. "I just know I can't."

My friend didn't say a word as we crossed the street and fetched our bikes and the circus posters. He kept his head down, like he didn't even care to look at me.

"Now what's gotten into *you?*" I asked, still in a huff.

He glanced at me, then commenced chomping the wad of gum in his mouth. "Well, gal, maybe you're chewing on the boy too much."

I felt anger flash inside me again. *"Me?* In case you didn't notice, *he's* the one who just got us into that mess."

Leo picked up his bike. "Yeah, but you've been mighty feisty since him and his pa showed up. You been actin' like a plumb different person."

I stiffened. "We're talking about Walter, not me. He's the one causing all the trouble."

"I ain't sayin' you caused anything, gal. It's jest —"

I jerked my bicycle up from the ground. "I don't want to talk about it. I'm tired and fed up is all."

Leo shrugged.

We continued tacking up posters along the street in an uneasy silence. I didn't care to think about whether I'd been too harsh on the boy like Leo said. But I knew one thing. We'd have to catch up to my cousin soon. It wasn't safe for man nor beast to leave him to himself.

When we reached the alley where we'd last seen Walter, we propped our bikes against the side of a building. I'd ridden my bike this way before. I knew the alley would dead end behind a drugstore and a cafe.

"Well, do we wait him out or go in and fetch him?" I asked Leo.

"We'd best go git 'im, gal," Leo said. "The way he was cryin', he might be in there all day."

"Don't let that phony sobbing fool you," I pointed out. "He faked plenty when I lived with the Tylers in Kansas."

Before we started down the alley, a man raced out wearing a wide-brimmed, brown hat tugged down low over his eyes. Wild, long black hair poked out from under the brim. He dodged us without looking our way and jumped into a dented, black Ford parked at the curb. The car sped away.

I turned to head back down the alley. But Leo dropped his circus posters to the ground and grabbed his bicycle.

"Leo?" I called as my friend hopped on his bike.

"Gotta—" Leo began, but I didn't hear the rest. He stood high on his pedals and commenced pumping that bike hard.

"Leo!" I cried. "Leo, what're—"

I didn't finish. He wouldn't have heard me anyway. He'd already raced half a block down the street after the Ford. I watched the car turn left. Seconds later Leo turned left after it. He was gone from sight.

What on earth had gotten into the boy? Why would Leo take off after that stranger? It made no sense.

Then out of the alley burst Walter. He ran smack into me.

"Hey!" I yelled, grabbing his arm. "What've you been up to in there?"

My cousin turned and stared wide-eyed down the empty alley. He gasped, "Don't think they saw me. I was hid pretty good."

"Walter!" I said, giving him a little shake. "What are you talking about?"

Suddenly he seemed to recognize me. He grabbed the strap of my overalls and held tight.

"Jessie, listen, there's—" he began. "Uh-oh." His eyes fixed on something in the alley.

I looked and spotted Rand Buchanan coming out. He
wore his holster and clutched his whip in one hand. With
the other he brushed imaginary dust off his white trou-
sers and touched his head like he wanted to make sure
each plastered-down black hair was in place. It was.

When the Great Buchanan spotted Walter and me, his
face darkened. He stopped in his tracks and stared at us.
Then his black eyebrows knitted together.

"I thought you kiddos had a job to do," he remarked
without flashing his usual bright smile.

"We've been working—see?" I said, pointing to the
few posters on the sidewalk. "They're mostly up already."

"What I see is you've still got some to go."

He didn't smile. He just stalked off like he had no
desire to lay eyes on the likes of us.

A cloud of worry came over me. The Great Buchanan
had just that morning practically promised Uncle Rudy a
job with the circus. I sure didn't want him mad at me. Not
now.

"We'll get right to work!" I called out after him.

If he heard me, he didn't answer. He just tramped up
the sidewalk, slapping his coiled whip against his leg and
not looking back.

Walter's hand still held tight to my clothes.

"Jessie, wait'll you hear what—"

I pushed my cousin away. "What kind of trouble did
you get into back there?"

He shook his head. "No trouble. He didn't see me

hiding. But I heard—"

"I don't care to hear any more of your lies."

"But Jessie," he whined.

"Stop whining and start tacking up posters," I ordered, fetching my bike. "You haven't done a lick of work yet."

"But I gotta tell you—"

"Hush up, Walter, and get busy. I'll be back in a few minutes, and I expect to find you working."

I climbed on my homemade bicycle and pushed away from the curb. Walter kept shouting at me. Something about what he'd heard in the alley. I didn't care to hear it. I had more important things on my mind. Like where Leo took off to. And why.

I pedaled down the street, turning left where I'd seen the car and Leo go. I kept going straight, stopping at every corner and glancing in both directions, hopeful I'd spy the dented, black Ford or Leo's red bike or the boy himself. I saw nothing.

Before long I smelled the fresh saltiness of the Pacific Ocean. Ahead, I spied the sign for the Santa Monica pier. Beneath it lay Leo's bike. My heart commenced to race. Where was—? Then I spotted the boy himself, leaning against the railing and staring out at the ocean. I sighed, relieved.

I pedaled out on the pier and jumped off my bike.

"Leo, what're you doing?" I asked.

He didn't budge, didn't answer. Just kept looking out at the endless blue waves. I glanced around. I didn't see the black Ford anywhere.

"Why'd you take off like that?" I asked.

"I lost him," Leo mumbled. He didn't look at me. He just kept staring at the ocean.

"Lost who?" I said.

The boy sighed and turned toward me. His face seemed stony, not like usual when he chomped gum and kept me company. The rope he always twirled hung forgotten at his side.

"The man in that car," he said in almost a whisper. "I think—" He licked his lips. "I think he was my pa."

I just stared at him.

"Your *pa?*" I said. "But he—he ran off when your brother died. You told me so yourself."

He looked right at me. His dark eyes glistened. "He did. I ain't seen him since. Leastwise till this mornin' at the circus."

"But you said your pa ran off in Colorado. Why would he be here?"

"Don't rightly know, gal. 'Less he's lookin' for me."

I shook my head. "That couldn't be. He doesn't know you're here."

"Well, I sent that one letter to my sister Nina after your folks took me in," he explained. "I figure he's talked to her."

I didn't want to believe one whit of it. I didn't want Leo's father to turn up. Not if it meant he might take my almost-brother away.

Leo rubbed his face with his hands. Then he looked at me and said, "Gal, I'm all mixed up. If it is Pa, should I yell at 'im for leavin' me? Or should I just grab hold an' stick with 'im for good?"

I held an opinion on that, but I kept my mouth shut. I sure didn't want to mix him up worse. Instead, I said, "You don't know for sure that it's even him."

"It sure 'nough looked like 'im. Even wore a wide-brimmed, brown hat same as Pa, down low over his eyes."

"Still, it could've been someone who just looked like him."

"But, gal, what if it *is* him?" he pleaded.

I had no answer. The two of us just stood there staring out at the ocean. After a while Leo shrugged and asked, "Where's Walter?"

"He's—" I stopped myself and jerked around to face Leo. "Oh, no. I left him back in town. He's supposed to be tacking up the rest of the posters."

"You left Walter alone with a hammer and a sack of tacks?" Leo said, looking at me like I was a plumb fool. Which I was.

Pictures flashed in my mind of what that spoiled nine-year-old might do with a hammer. Not a citizen in all of Santa Monica was safe now.

Chapter 8

We pedaled furiously back to the spot where I'd left Walter. The boy, of course, was nowhere in sight. The hammers, tacks, and posters lay untouched on the sidewalk. My cousin still hadn't done a lick of work.

I got off my bike, plopped down on the ground, and groaned. I felt plumb worn out from chasing after Leo and now Walter again.

"Gal, sorry my runnin' off like that made you lose track of 'im," Leo said with a sheepish glance at me. He stooped over to collect the posters.

"Not your fault," I replied, but in my heart I only halfway meant it.

We stayed like that for a spell. I sat and rested, unable to get up the gumption to start searching again. Leo hugged the posters close and appeared lost in thought.

After a while he said, "What if that man turns out to be my pa? Whatcha think I oughta do?"

I glanced up at him. It troubled me to see this Leo. A Leo who didn't twirl a rope, who didn't chomp gum.

"I can't tell you what to do," I said, trying to sound cheerful. But I really wanted to say: *Stay away from that man! He left you flat once. He's plain undependable.*

"Yeah, but what would *you* do?"

He turned his dark eyes on me. His wild black hair shot up in all sorts of directions. He bit his lip and waited for me to answer.

What should I say? I didn't want to remind him that only weeks ago I'd crossed half the country to find Mama and Daddy. That I thought being with my parents was one of the most important things in this world. Instead, I just said, "Strikes me he's not too dependable."

Leo frowned, seeming to mull over my words. Then he said, "But he's still my pa, ain't he?"

I turned my head away. I didn't want him to see the anger and fear I felt. Anger at this man who might be Leo's pa. Fear that he might take my almost-brother away.

I reached for the hammer and tacks. "Let's finish up and find Walter," I said, changing the subject. I couldn't bear thinking about Leo and the stranger anymore.

An hour later, with all the posters up, we hadn't gotten so much as a glimpse of Walter. We rode our bikes one more time up and down the streets of Santa Monica. There was no sign of him.

Finally, we headed back to the circus. And that was where we caught up with him at last.

No sooner had we ridden onto the circus grounds than I spied Walter outside a small, green tent. Gold crescent moons and stars and such decorated the canvas. Strings of colored glass beads hung down in the doorway. Tied between two poles a cloth sign flapped beside the tent's entrance.

Madame Gaspar
knows all, tells all
Your Fortune Revealed—5 cents

A fortune-teller! If that didn't beat all. The boy had no business in there.

I yelled, *"Walter!"*

He heard me and his arm jerked back just as he reached out to part the glass beads. Like a kid caught stealing candy from a jar. This kid, though, didn't stop. He turned and smirked at me, then slipped through the beads.

"Oh no!" I exclaimed. "The heathens're about to get ahold of my cousin! We can't let him go in there."

"Looks like he's already done it, gal," Leo answered.

I pushed off and raced my bike across the field to the tent of Madame Gaspar. My skin crawled just thinking of Walter in such a place.

Hopping off my bike, I stopped at the entrance to the tent. I didn't want to go inside. I knew I shouldn't. But how else could I get Walter out?

Leo came up and grabbed my arm. "Gal, I think I saw 'im over there!"

"Walter? He's in here—"

"No, Pa!" he exclaimed.

"Leo, Walter's in this lion's den and you want to run off

after some stranger." I refused to think of the man as Leo's pa.

"I jest got this feelin' he might be lookin' for me."

"Well, if he is your pa, he's not very observant," I replied crossly. "He ran right past us when he came out of that alley."

While Leo mulled that over, I took a deep breath, parted the tinkling glass beads with my fingertips, and slipped inside the tent.

At first I couldn't see a thing owing to the dim light. Then my eyes adjusted, and I sure didn't like what I saw. Not one whit.

Walter sat on a wooden box on one side of a squatty table. The table held a glass ball that gave off a strange, milky kind of light. Hunched over the other side of the table I made out a woman wearing a long, dark robe.

"Walter—"

"*Shhhhhhh!*" the woman warned.

"I will not be shushed by a fortune-teller," I informed her.

Her head shot up. The fortune-teller wore lots of makeup on her eyes and her lipstick smeared considerable beyond her mouth. Several glittery chains and necklaces dangled from her neck, and bracelets clanked on her wrists. She jangled something fierce every time she moved. But the makeup and jewelry didn't fool me. This was no Madame anyone. Her face and hands looked young. She reminded me of a little girl playing dress-up. Madame Gaspar indeed!

She commenced waving her hands around the phony crystal ball. She had pudgy kid's fingers with plenty of rings and her nails were painted bright red.

"Magic ball, reveal the secrets from the future," she crooned. "What do the fates have in store for Walter?"

The fates! I was all set to give this phony mystic a piece of my mind when Leo rushed through the beaded doorway and bumped into me.

"What's goin' on in here, gal?" he said.

"*Shhhhh!*" the girl warned again, not even bothering to look up this time.

"Walter, you come out of here this instant," I demanded.

Both Walter and the fortune-teller ignored me. I knew I should've just grabbed that boy and yanked him off the box, but something stopped me. Phony or not, the girl spooked me some, what with the way she reached over that ball and talked to it and all.

"The picture from the future is coming clearer now," the girl sang out. "I see. . . . "

"What do ya see?" my cousin asked eagerly.

"I see you as famous, known throughout the world."

Leo leaned close and whispered in my ear, "Yeah, famous like Billy the Kid."

"Gee, what will I be famous for?" Walter said.

"That much is not revealed," the fortune teller replied. "But fame and wealth will come to you."

"I reckon a bank robber *would* git plenty wealthy, wouldn't he?" Leo speculated in a whisper.

The girl spun around and pointed her fat finger right at me. "You, dear. The one with the poor opinion of seers. You're next."

"Oh no I'm not," I declared. I looked at Walter and threatened, "If you hand this person a nickel, I will personally bop you on the head."

"No, my dear," the fortune-teller said. "This consultation is free. For a more detailed viewing of the future, he can come back when the circus opens. For a mere five pennies his future will be fully revealed."

Hogwash! I stepped over to Walter and yanked him up.

"*Owww!* You're hurtin' me!"

"You come along right now," I warned. "Before you get into any more trouble."

As I pulled my cousin through the glass beads, I heard the girl say, "And what about you, young man? No charge. Just a glimpse into what is and what will be."

I spun around. *Leo!*

"Well, I don't rightly see harm in it," Leo replied.

"Leo, don't do it!" I warned.

"Young lady, remove yourself before I'm forced to call upon the unseen forces!"

I stood just outside and peeked through the beads. I saw Leo sit on the box. Then the girl started waving her hands over the glowing crystal ball again. Walter struggled to free himself, but I held on tight. I wouldn't make the sorry mistake of turning him loose again.

"I see—"

"You'd best see that boy getting up on his two feet and

clearing out of there," I declared through the doorway.

The girl commenced screeching some kind of high-pitched mumbo jumbo that made Leo jump. I had to admit, it gave me the jitters too. Was she calling on those unseen forces she'd made mention of?

"Please, gal, jest simmer down," Leo called to me, staying put on that box.

I could see he had his mind set on getting his fortune told, though I couldn't for the life of me figure out why.

The girl continued her mumbo jumbo. "Oh, magic ball, open the future like a door and let us walk through."

The very idea!

"Aha!" she sang out like a delighted child. "I'm beginning to see something. Some shadow."

"Where?" Leo asked, leaning over the milky ball.

"Patience, boy," the girl crooned. "It's— No, it isn't you. Someone perhaps looking for you. I see a possible reunion in your future."

"Reunion?" Leo said, frowning.

"With someone you know."

"My pa!" Leo cried. He twisted and looked at me, his dark eyes shining.

The fool boy. Not five minutes ago we'd talked about his pa right outside the tent. That girl was no more a fortune-teller than I was President Roosevelt.

Then the phony told Leo, "Come back when the circus opens for a full, complete reading. Only five cents."

"Come on, Leo." I stomped away from the tent, yanking Walter after me.

I climbed on my bike and made Walter sit on the handlebars. Before I could push off, Leo stepped out of the tent. He picked up his bike from the ground. Glancing back, I saw the girl peek through the beaded doorway. In the daylight, she looked not much older than me.

I turned to Leo and said loud enough for the phony fortune-teller to hear me, "Fortune telling goes against the Bible. You'd best stay clear of this place. Besides, Madame Gaspar's only about twelve years old. She can't tell you anything about the future. She's barely had a past."

We pedaled away, bumping across the rutted field.

As we got back into town, the ride became considerable less bumpy. Walter said, "Jessie, I gotta tell you somethin'. In the alley this mornin', I heard that man—"

"Just don't talk to me," I interrupted, still put out with my cousin.

"But I heard him say—"

"Heard who? What on earth are you talking about?"

"That animal trainer. The Great Buchanan. He said—"

"Forget it, Walter," I snapped. "It's likely none of your business."

Leo pedaled silently beside us. Twice he nearly slammed into cars parked in the street. This bothered me. Leo could ride most anything, even bucking broncos I figured. What on earth did he have his mind set on?

After a time he said, "You know, gal, I think maybe that man *is* my pa."

So that was it. He'd let that phony fortune-teller convince him the stranger was his father.

"Don't believe what that girl told you," I said. "She just heard us talking outside the tent is all."

"I don't care, gal. I've gotta— I've gotta—"

I gripped the handlebars tight. *Why can't he see the truth? Why is he so befuddled? Didn't his father run out on him and leave him flat?*

All of a sudden Leo skidded his bike to a stop. I stopped too.

"Gal, I've gotta go back to the circus."

"It can wait till after lunch," I said.

"Nope. Nope it can't wait," he answered as he turned his bike around and hightailed it toward the circus.

Of all things!

Well, let him go. Let him believe that ridiculous fortune-teller if he wanted to. Let him run after some man who ran away from him in the first place. Just let him go.

Chapter 9

That night, after I washed up the supper dishes, I took my pet armadillo, Victoria, and plopped myself down on the front step. I wanted to get away from all the hubbub in the house. I still felt fit to be tied, as Daddy would say. And I didn't want to talk to anyone just then.

Leo hadn't come home till supper time. The food was already laid out when he dropped into the chair next to mine. He muttered, "Didn't find him, gal." I knew he meant the man he took to be his father. Said he'd ridden his bike all over but never laid eyes on him again. Saw the Great Buchanan though. The animal trainer'd been practicing his act for a man in a brown suit and shoes with white spats.

Cradling Victoria in my lap, I thought about Leo's fruitless search. I said to her, "What'd he expect? That a man who'd run out on him once would suddenly turn up and want him back? He's got a new family and a new home. Isn't that enough?"

Home? The word stuck in my head. We had us a nice house all right. A real mansion compared to the tarpaper shacks we'd lived in when Daddy sharecropped in Oklahoma. But those shacks felt more like home than this place.

All because Uncle Rudy'd taken over my room, leaving
me to sleep on the couch in the living room. All because I
never got a moment's peace with Walter about. It just
wasn't fair.

I heard the front screen door squeak open. Looking
back, I made out the dark shape of Daddy in the yellow
rectangle of the door. I turned back around and tried to
peer out into the black night.

Daddy eased himself down next to me on the porch
step. Like someone getting used to the cold water in a
swimming hole.

"Grand night out, isn't it, Jess?" he said once he got
settled. He reached out and scratched Victoria's nose.

"I guess," I mumbled.

"Where's Leo?"

"Don't know," I answered. But in my head I thought,
Probably off looking for his runaway father.

I felt Daddy's eyes on me. I didn't look his way.

"What's wrong?" he asked.

"Nothing."

"Don't sound too convincing."

Suddenly I didn't think I could keep everything bottled
inside me anymore. I spun around and said, "Walter was
nothing but a pest today."

I told him about the disaster at the circus and how
Walter's slingshot had gotten us in hot water with the
owner. About the trouble at the warehouse when my
cousin had put up the "Now Hiring" sign. How the sheriff
had falsely accused me. And about dragging Walter out of

the fortune-teller's tent.

"Sounds like you've had a hard day," he admitted.

"Looks like I'm in for a whole summer of hard days."

"Not so loud, honey," he cautioned.

"Well, Daddy, it's just not fair. I can't sleep in my own bed. And I saw the big mess in my bedroom. Uncle Rudy's got his stuff scattered all over the floor. He didn't even make my bed. Looks like he's fixing to be here a long time."

Daddy patted my knee. "It'll only be for a bit, Jess. Just till he finds work."

"Well, when's he going to start looking? Mama said herself he stayed in bed till almost noon. He didn't even shave today."

"Well, Rudy's not much of an early riser, I'll grant you that."

"Mama said he didn't even go out looking for work this afternoon."

"We've gotta give him some time, honey," Daddy said.

Time? Time to lounge around the house all day complaining about the bank in Liberal taking away his gas station? Time to send for Aunt Edna and the rest of the Tylers? Like Leo'd said, Uncle Rudy seemed to like living off the fat of the Lands.

"Times are hard, even in California," Daddy reminded me.

I knew he was right. I just didn't want to admit it, so I changed the subject.

"But Walter. He's driving me crazy. He's nothing but a

troublemaker—and a big brat to boot. And Uncle Rudy doesn't lift a finger to set him straight."

Daddy sighed. "Well, Jess, I know Walter can be a peck of trouble. But the Lord wants us to help others in times of need. And I can't imagine a greater time of need in this country than right now. Are you too proud to help someone else, a blood kin no less?"

"Yessir. I mean nosir."

"I know it doesn't seem fair to you, giving up your room and watching after Walter. But it's only for a time."

"How long a time?" I asked, though I wasn't sure I'd find the answer to my liking.

"Depends on Rudy I reckon."

"That's what bothers me."

"Meanwhile, you and Leo keep watching after Walter, you hear? I know I can trust you to do the right thing."

"Yessir," I answered softly. I had no choice.

Daddy leaned over and gave me a peck on the cheek. "That's my Jess."

Then he patted Victoria on her armored spine and got to his feet. He went inside. The squeak of the screen door went right up and down my back and made me flinch.

I sat there for a while thinking about what Daddy'd said. Maybe I *had* been too harsh on Uncle Rudy and Walter, considering the hard times and all. I tried not to think about my room, or Walter's shenanigans.

Before long I heard something. A sniffling sound coming from the side yard. I glanced back inside the house.

Uncle Rudy and Mama sat together talking on the couch. Walter crawled on the floor acting like a wild circus animal. Daddy sat reading in a chair.

The sniffling came again.

Leo?

It sounded like the faint kind of whimper boys'll make sometimes when they're trying hard not to cry.

I wanted to sneak off the porch and slip away so Leo wouldn't see me. I didn't want to embarrass him by catching him crying. I tried to ease off the step, but the boards creaked.

The sniffling stopped.

"Who's there?" Leo's voice rang out. "Gal, is that you?"

I hugged Victoria close in my arms. Then I tiptoed around the other side of the house as quiet as I could manage.

"Who's there?" Leo called out in the dark behind me.

I waited a bit. Then I yelled, "Hey, Leo, where are you?" I returned to the front of the house and up to the porch where the boy now stood.

"Hey, Leo."

Light from inside spilled out around him, turning my friend into a black shape.

"What're you doin'?" he asked as I came up and stood beside him. I could make out his face now. If he'd cried any tears, he'd since wiped them away.

"Just out walking," I said. It wasn't much of a lie.

He scratched his wild hair and eyed me suspiciously.

Then he shrugged and we sat on the steps where I'd been before. Victoria tucked her pointed head under my arm and settled back in my lap.

"I even checked the soup kitchens and the men standin' in lines for jobs," Leo said.

He still had his mind fixed on that man, the one he took to be his father.

"Well, it probably isn't him," I said. "I can't for the life of me see how your pa'd show up here."

I wanted to add, *And I don't want him to show up. You're part of my family now. Just forget about him!* But I held my tongue.

"Don't know, gal. It sure looked like 'im. Specially wearin' that hat that way and all."

Leo's brooding irritated me. I wanted to steer his mind off the subject. I said, "Daddy told me there's a new foal over at Mr. Rogers' ranch. Maybe we can go take a look at it."

He shrugged.

"I just don't want Walter along," I complained. "Mr. Rogers says he never met a man he didn't like. But he's never met Walter."

"You're right there, gal," he said, looking away.

"Well, I'm praying that circus job pans out for Uncle Rudy. Then maybe they'll be gone in a few days."

"Maybe," Leo said. I could tell he wasn't giving Walter, the circus, or the new foal any thought.

Suddenly I felt fed up with his moodiness. I burst out, "I wish you'd quit thinking about your pa. Here he ran out on you and broke up your family and all you've been doing is moping around. Wishing you could be with him."

I felt Leo's dark eyes on me. He didn't say a word. He didn't need to. I'd already said it all.

After the longest time he spoke up, his voice shaky. "It's easy for you. You got a pa. A durn good one. All I wanna do—"

"Leo, don't you see? *You* got a pa too! Mama and Daddy love you like you're their own flesh-and-blood son."

"Doncha think I know that, gal?" he said, his voice rising in the dark. "Doncha think I'm grateful? I am. I've never known a family like yours before. I don't wanna give it up. But what if this man's my real pa, gal? Shouldn't I *want* to be with 'im?"

His question haunted me. "Are you saying you *don't* want to be with him?"

He shrugged. "I'm jest flustered and perplexed is what I am. I wanna meet up with 'im and find out why he took off the way he did. Maybe if he had a good reason, maybe then I might wanna...." His voice trailed off.

All of sudden I felt about as low as a drove-over snake. Poor Leo. He was plumb confused. He didn't want to go back to his father, but he felt like he ought to. All my jawing at him had been pure selfishness. I had to help him, to make it up to him somehow.

I remembered the faceless man with the wide-brimmed hat darting out of the alley. Then I remembered the rest of it. I got an idea. "Leo! After he came out of that alley this morning, I saw the Great Buchanan too. Maybe he knows that man. You could ask him leastwise."

Leo sat up suddenly. "Yeah! Thanks, gal! That's a right good idea."

He started to get up, but I pulled him back down.

"Wait. Not tonight. It's late. It'll keep till tomorrow."

He relaxed. "I guess you're right. I'll talk to him in the mornin' over at the circus." He popped a stick of gum into his mouth and commenced chomping.

Yes, the circus, I thought. It had been the one bright spot in the coming days. If only my cousin hadn't taken aim at that elephant's rear with his slingshot. If only we didn't have to work off the damages. If only. . . .

I felt a tinge of anger rise up in me.

Crash!

I jumped. The sound of glass breaking came from inside the house. Then again, another crash!

Leo and I looked at each other. What had Walter broken now?

Together we bolted to our feet and charged through the front door to find out.

Chapter 10

When we got to the circus early the next morning, Leo kept looking around for the Great Buchanan. He asked Cami Starr where the animal trainer might be. She just told him, "Haven't seen him yet."

The circus owner's work shirt and jeans looked grimier than yesterday. Patches of dried mud clung to the knees of her faded pants. Her gray hat seemed even more crumpled. A tangle of dark hair swept down over her eyes, and dirt and sweat streaked her cheek. She looked like she'd worked through the night and hadn't cleaned up a bit. The red megaphone still hung around her neck, but at least she didn't use it on us that morning.

She led us to six white Arabian horses tethered to a rope between a couple of trees. The horses stirred as we walked behind them.

Patting the flank of one mare, Cami Starr said, "Brush them good. And wash their legs too. We can't have our ring stock looking like this. You'll find a water trough on the other side of the stripe's cage."

Walter groaned. "We already worked enough to pay for that crummy bleacher," he muttered.

I spun around. "Leo and I worked plenty yesterday.

Can't say the same for you." I warned my cousin, "But
you'd better do your share today."

Cami Starr turned on her boot heels and walked off.
Not even a trace of a smile had crossed her tired face.

"Right friendly lady," Leo quipped.

"She's got a load on her mind, I suspect," I said.

Leo and I grabbed brushes and got to work. Walter
sauntered over to a nearby truck and leaned against it. He
toyed with his slingshot some, then stuck it back in his
pocket. He commenced kicking up dirt with the toe of his
shoe. I tried to be patient, but the boy's lack of industry
riled me.

"Walter, come over here," I yelled.

He took his time doing it, meandering this way and
that. When he finally stood in front of me, I stooped and
plucked up a dented metal pail.

"Make yourself useful and go fetch a bucket of water,"
I told him as cheerfully as I could manage.

"Why me?" he grumbled, not reaching for the pail.

I had half a mind to box the boy's ears. Instead, I said
with a fake sweetness in my voice, "Because you're not
doing anything better. And because I told you to."

"Phoo, you ain't the boss of me," he sassed.

So much for sweetness. I gave him a harsh look and
shoved the pail into his hands. He took it and headed off.
Leo shouted after him, "Keep an eye out for the Great
Buchanan, will ya?"

Walter swung the pail around as he disappeared around
the big top.

"We'll likely not see him for a while," Leo speculated.

"We'd better," I threatened.

As the morning wore on, it began to heat up. I worked myself into a good sweat combing out the snags in the Arabians' manes and tails and giving their coats a good brushing. Beside me, Leo didn't speak. I figured he was planning what to say to the man he took to be his pa.

Every so often I'd stop with the horses and watch the circus folks going past. Dressed in regular clothes, they looked like normal people. But the things they did were strange and wonderful. I saw a man juggling five bottles in the air. And he didn't drop a one! A woman rode past sitting high atop an elephant. Then a man and woman danced by with a whole slew of folks balanced on their shoulders!

When Leo and I finished grooming the horses, Walter still hadn't returned with the water.

"I knew I couldn't trust that boy to do a simple job," I declared. "I'm sick of spending all my time looking for him."

"I don't much like the idea of him roamin' 'round with that slingshot," Leo replied.

Oh, no—the slingshot! How could I have forgotten it? *Lord, please don't let that boy wreck anything else.* I sure didn't want to work the rest of my life paying for his pranks.

We set down our brushes and headed in the direction of the water trough. As we walked across the sun-baked ground, smells drifted toward me. The heavy, ripe scents of animals and old canvas. And hot dogs cooking at what Cami Starr called the "grease joint." From the other side of the big top came the sounds of people shouting and laughing and hammers pounding. These smells and sounds combined to make the circus like no other place I knew.

When I spotted the big cats' cages ahead, we slowed. I noticed the lions pacing back and forth. Their uneasiness spooked me. I wanted to shake my fear. But it hung on.

Then I spied him. Walter. What I saw sent a chill up my back. Dear Lord!

"Leo, *look!*" I cried.

"I see, gal," he gasped.

We watched as Walter reached for the latch on the tiger's cage! The little fool had brains made of mush.

I took off running toward my cousin. *"Walter! Stop!"* I yelled. "Walter!"

The boy whipped around with a look of surprise. I'd caught him red-handed all right. I dashed up to him and grabbed his shirt. It seemed like I'd been yanking on his shirt since the moment he stepped off the train.

"Walter, what do you think you're doing?" I demanded.

Leo ran up behind me. He poked me. "Gal, that cage door—"

I pulled away. "Not now, Leo. And quit poking me. I've got this knothead here."

"But—"

"Later, Leo!" I snapped. I got a good grip on my cousin. He struggled against me. "You thought it'd be funny to let the tiger out, is that it?" I gave him a good shake.

"That ain't it 'tall, Jessie Land," Walter protested. "That cage was open I tell ya. I was just cl—"

"Don't lie to me, Walter," I said. "Who'd go around leaving the cages open?"

"But I didn't do it," Walter cried. "It was—"

"I should've never let you out of my sight," I said, giving the boy another shake. Over my shoulder I told Leo, "Good thing we came along when we did."

"Gal, will ya listen to me," Leo pleaded. "The cage. It *is* open!"

What'd he say? The cage. . . . Even looking past Walter and seeing for myself, I still couldn't believe it. The tiger's cage was unlatched!

I froze. I stared through the bars at the tiger. He stared back at me. I swallowed—hard. "Leo, we've gotta close that door," I said softly. "And quick."

"Whattaya think I was tryin' to do?" Walter grumbled.

I ignored the little pest, keeping my mind on how to get that cage door latched. I said, "OK, on three, we push the cage door all the way closed. Then I'll latch it while you two hold it tight."

The cage sat only two steps away, but it may as well have been a mile. The tiger stood in the far corner watching us. His yellow eyes burned as if they were glowing with anger. He opened his mouth wide, baring those sharp, pointed teeth. Teeth that could rip a person to shreds.

"One . . . " I began. I let go of Walter's shirt.

"Two . . . " I took a deep breath and tried not to look at the tiger.

"Three!" All three of us leaped forward and grabbed the bars of the cage. The iron door clanged, its ringing hammering in my head.

"The *latch!*" Leo yelled. "Get the latch, gal!"

Just as I reached up to bolt the door, the tiger sprang forward, throwing his weight against the bars. The door swung out, knocking the three of us flat on the ground.

For a moment we lay still. Above us the tiger stood poised. He opened his mouth. Tiger saliva dripped onto my leg. A loud roar exploded in the air. I shut my eyes and prayed, *Lord, don't let him eat us!*

Then he shot out. With one long leap, he flew over us. I watched his orange, black, and white stripes soar against the bright blue sky. It was kind of pretty, save for us being under him and all. My heart pounded in my chest. I gasped for air. I twisted around and saw Attila race around the corner of the circus tent.

The big cat had escaped!

Then I heard something else. A terrible creak. The sound of metal scraping against metal. I rolled over in time to see one of the lions put its large furry head against its cage door. The door swung wide. One after another, the two lions leaped out. For a moment they stood still.

Then they headed for us.

Chapter 11

The lions growled, then stepped closer. My brain told my legs to run, but they stayed frozen stiff. Walter crouched behind me, hiding.

"Don't let 'em get me, Jessie!" he whimpered.

"You shouldn't have opened those cage doors," I snapped.

"But—but I didn't!" he sobbed. I felt the back of my shirt grow damp from his tears. "I saw—"

"Hush up, Walter," I said, feeling angry and fearful all at the same time. I had to think what to do.

"Gal, just stay still," Leo cautioned, edging closer.

I did as he said, trusting his instinct with animals. I remembered the wolf we'd faced a couple of weeks ago. That had scared me plenty. But these lions were another thing. They made that angry wolf seem like a house pet.

I knew I had to do something quick. My gaze fixed on the door to the tiger's cage. It still stood open, giving me an idea. It might just work. If it didn't, we'd like as not end up lion vittles.

"Quick, get inside the tiger's cage," I told the two boys huddled against me.

"Gal, what're ya plannin'?" Leo gasped.

There was no time to explain. "Just do it."

"*Nooooo,*" moaned Walter. "I don't wanna be trapped in no tiger's cage."

"Go on," I urged. "Nice and easy. No sudden moves."

Just a few feet away the lions crouched low, sniffing the air. They looked alert and ready to pounce in any direction.

Leo went first. He edged over to the empty cage and slowly climbed inside. Then he turned and reached for Walter.

"No-no-no-no-no," my cousin groaned, but he let Leo pull him in.

I reached for the door. The lions moved toward me.

"Hurry, gal," Leo urged.

Then one of the lions darted forward. *Dear Lord, keep me safe like You did Daniel!*

In that instant, Cami Starr popped out from between two circus trucks. She held a small stool in one hand and a long cane in the other. "Keep still!" she yelled.

For the life of me I wanted to climb in that cage and clang the door shut. But I didn't move.

"Back, girl," Cami Starr said. She held the stool in front of her chest and poked at the lion with the long cane. "Get back, Ginger!"

Ginger didn't much cotton to being directed where to go. Letting loose a roar that made me shiver, she stood her ground, slapping at the cane. I tried to swallow. My throat felt as dry as a dusty Oklahoma road.

The lion kept batting at the cane and growling. But Cami Starr didn't give up. Step by step she coaxed Ginger toward her cage. The other lion, the one with the big, bushy mane, crouched low, watching with a kind of nervous look. Then, with one smooth motion, Ginger leaped back into her cage. The second lion jumped in right after her.

"Good, Fred!" the circus owner called out.

Fred and Ginger. I sank to the ground. She'd named her lions after famous moving-picture stars.

I watched as Cami Starr latched the door tight. I wanted to get up, but my legs felt too wobbly to hold me. Then the Great Buchanan appeared out of nowhere. He held his whip and pistol just like always.

"I see I'm too late," he remarked.

Cami Starr eyed him. "Attila's loose."

"What?" he exclaimed, glancing at the tiger cage where Leo and Walter still huddled. "Where'd he go?"

Leo and Walter scrambled out of the cage. I stood up beside them.

"I've no idea," the circus owner said. "But I have a notion these three lotlice might know something."

She dropped the stool and pointed at us with the cane. I saw fire in her eyes. She yanked up the megaphone that hung from her neck and yelled at us, "What've you kids done now? Why are you even here? These cages are *off-limits!*"

"We—we—we were looking for Walter," I stammered.

"I didn't do nothin'!" Walter protested. "Those doors were open when I got here."

The Great Buchanan stepped up behind Cami Starr. He

slapped his leg with the coiled whip.

"It was —" I started to explain.

"Quiet!" Cami Starr shouted through the megaphone. "No time to talk." She pointed to the right. "Rand, go that way. I'll circle around. Let's hope the stripe didn't go far."

The Great Buchanan nodded and rushed off. Cami Starr threw us another hard look and declared, "I'll deal with you three later." Then she disappeared around the big top.

I shut my eyes and rubbed my face. More trouble. This time it wasn't just a broken bleacher. A tiger'd escaped! My head hurt as I recalled Cami Starr's hard look and her anger. And what about the Great Buchanan? I sure didn't want him mad at me. That might ruin Uncle Rudy's chance at a circus job. There'd been trouble and more trouble, ever since — since Walter arrived.

I felt anger well up in me all over again. Walter was the one. He'd brought on all this trouble. I grabbed him by his collar and yelled, *"Now* look what you did!"

Walter tried to yank himself free. "I tol' ya. I *didn't* do it!"

"Lies, lies, lies," I spat, holding him close. "I'm sick and tired of your lies. You've gone too far now. You'll be punished for this."

My cousin jerked free and ran. He turned back once and screamed, "I didn't do it! Why're ya always blamin' me?"

He raced off in the direction the Great Buchanan had

gone. The very same direction Attila had gone.

"Walter, come back!" I shouted.

I shook my head and glanced at Leo. He said nothing. But I could tell by the look of disappointment on his face that he figured I'd been too hard on the boy.

"Well, I'm just plain fed up," I said to him, sticking up for myself.

"I know, but now we gotta go after 'im agin," Leo sighed. "You may not care if that tiger gits aholt of him, but I 'spect his pa won't 'preciate it none." He set off after my cousin, not even looking back to see if I'd follow.

I knew Leo was right. Like it or not, I'd been put in charge of Walter. I took off after Leo, feeling low and mad at the same time. I thought, *Lord, don't let Walter run into that tiger. Even if he does deserve it!*

When we got to the other side of the big top, we found folks running in all directions. Some shouted warnings like, "Tiger on the loose!" Or "Run for your life!" It frightened me to see the circus folks acting so scared. I saw the Great Buchanan with his gun and whip peek into the big top. Then he darted inside. I glimpsed Cami Starr race behind a row of trucks.

Then I spied Walter. He lit out across the lot, headed for a field of parked cars.

"Walter!" I cried. But the boy didn't stop or look back. He just kept running.

"Come on," I told Leo.

We chased after my cousin.

By the time we reached the cars, Walter had vanished

again. I spun around looking for him.

"Where'd he go?" I gasped, bending over to catch my breath.

"Dunno," Leo said, chomping his gum and scratching his head.

Then I spied something else. Not Walter, but trouble just the same. A sleek orange and black shape, sliding low between the closely parked cars. *The tiger!* His yellow eyes flickered in the bright sunlight as he glanced our way.

"Uh-oh," Leo remarked.

We ducked behind a black Essex, like the one my parents owned. Except this one had all its fenders.

I peeked around the back of the car. The tiger had started moving toward us.

"Gotta hide," I gasped, grabbing Leo's shirt. "Come on. In here."

I tugged on the back door handle of the Essex. It opened. I lurched inside, pulling Leo in after me. He slammed the door behind us. We huddled together on the floorboard, not daring to speak a word.

Through the open car window I heard the dry grass crunch as the tiger passed by. And I heard a kind of throaty rattle. The sound cats make when they purr, only louder. This, though, was no kitty cat. And I wouldn't call that sound purring. I remembered Attila's paws. As big as my head. Maybe bigger. And sharp teeth long as my fingers. I planned to stay on the floor of the car for a good long while.

After a time, though, Leo fidgeted. He whispered,

"Think it's safe?"

I heard people shouting in the distance.

"Let's keep still a while yet," I cautioned him.

It grew awful hot down there with the two of us cramped together. My legs and back began feeling stiff and tired from not moving. I was all set to get up when I heard something.

A man's voice. It grew louder till I could clearly hear his words. "Where'd that cat get to anyway?"

A deeper voice said, "Dunno."

I didn't recognize either voice. Then for a while I didn't hear anything. I glanced up. A man leaned against the front door of the Essex, his back to me. He wore a wrinkled brown suit and had short cropped hair the same color as his clothes.

I ducked back down. The man in the brown suit chuckled nervously. "He was right after all. Made it look like that kid let the cat go. *Ha!* A kid did the dirty work for ya."

The deep voice replied, "Missed those lions though. Coulda used them."

"The tiger'll have to do," the man in the brown suit said. "Ya just gotta catch that stripe for our circus. Be money in your pocket."

Leo tried to peek. "Who—"

I hushed him and pulled him down.

"Two thousand bucks, right?" the deep voice said.

Brown Suit replied, "You gotta catch him first. And not get caught yourself." He laughed that nervous little laugh again.

The other man mumbled something I couldn't make out.

"Take the stripe out to that abandoned house east of town," Brown Suit said. "Remember?"

The other man grunted.

"I'll meet you there."

The other man said something low.

"Already told ya," Brown Suit replied. "My uncle owns the circus. I'll see to it ya both get jobs. We get the stripe, it's a sure thing."

Leo pushed up from the floor for another peek. At once he dropped back down, his mouth open and his eyes wide.

I frowned at him.

"My *pa*," he whispered.

"Shhhh," I warned.

"My pa," he whispered again. "He's a *crook*."

I wanted to tell him he'd been mistaken. But it was clear these men were up to no good. I tried to think of a plan. Now we needed to do more than just find Walter. The men, though, stayed put, right by the Essex.

"Leo, we've got to get out of here and warn Cami Starr," I whispered.

He gave me a strange look. Like he couldn't believe I wanted to snitch on his father. But then he nodded, like he realized it was the right thing to do.

I waited a good long while. Then I glanced up and saw the two men had moved a couple of paces away from the Essex. I nodded to Leo and we scooted close to the door. I reached up and grasped the door handle. It felt cool in my sweaty hand. I pulled down. The little click it made sounded like a cannon going off in my ears.

"*Care*ful, gal," Leo whispered.

I pushed the door. It didn't make a sound and I smiled. But as it swung wide, I lost my grip. The door banged into the side of the car parked next to it. *Thud!*

I scampered out of the car and glanced back. The two men had heard the racket all right. The man in the brown suit reached in through the open window of the Essex and grabbed Leo's leg.

"*Gotcha!*" he cried.

Chapter 12

Leo kicked and struggled. I reached in and grabbed his arm, trying to free him from Brown Suit's grip. But the man held him tight. Through the window I saw the other man—the one Leo took to be his father—start around the car. Toward me!

With the door still open, I leaned into the back seat. Brown Suit's face loomed in front of me. He wore spectacles, and his scruffy moustache twitched under his large red nose. He gritted his tiny yellow teeth as he fought to get both hands on Leo. Just then Leo jabbed the man's hand with his free foot.

The man jerked back and screamed, *"Yow!"*

I grabbed Leo's arm and tugged him out of the car. We sprinted across the field for the big top. I heard the men yell, but I didn't stop till we got to the entrance of the tent. Then, panting, my heart throbbing, I glanced back.

"They're running off," I gasped, watching the two men dodge between the parked cars and head the other way.

Suddenly Leo's dark eyes grew fearful. He reached out and clutched the strap of my overalls. "Gal, my pa and that other man are *crooks*. You heard 'em. They're out to steal that tiger and sell it to some other circus."

"You sure he's your father?" I asked, still gasping.

"Looks like 'im, but I can't tell for sure 'cause o' that hat," he confessed, still breathing hard.

I didn't know what to say. What could you say to your best friend whose father turned out to be a crook? "Leo, I'm sorry."

He turned away. I saw one of his hands go up and wipe his face. I felt my heart break. I hoped to goodness that man wasn't his pa. Truly I did. The boy deserved better.

I glanced around. The circus lot looked deserted.

"Listen, we've got to tell someone what those men are up to," I said.

Leo turned to me. The streaks of dirt on his face told me he'd shed some tears. "Reckon so." He added, "And find Walter too."

Yes. Walter. I didn't want to admit I'd completely forgotten the boy.

"And find Walter," I agreed. "Come on."

Just then the canvas flap of the big top flew up. Out stepped the Great Buchanan. Thank goodness!

The animal trainer's eyes darted around and his dark face looked troubled. He wore the kind of look you'd expect on a man who'd just lost a tiger.

His gray eyes settled on us. "So, have you seen him?"

I knew he meant the tiger. I shook my head. "No, but we've gotta tell you something," I said. I explained about the two men and the plot to steal the tiger and sell it to another circus.

The Great Buchanan frowned and stroked his dark jaw.

When I finished, he shook his head.

"I just knew trouble was brewing," he said. "I'll bet Cami herself let those animals loose, not that boy."

"Cami Starr!" I exclaimed. "But why would—"

"She never wanted this circus to succeed," he declared. "She's sabotaged it before, back when the colonel was alive. Let a bear loose, though I could never prove it."

"What should we do?" I asked, though it troubled me to think of Cami Starr plotting to steal her own tiger.

The Great Buchanan glanced around. He pointed in the direction of the gas balloon. "Over there. I saw Johnny Tin Plate go that direction a little while ago."

"Johnny Tin Plate?" I said, not understanding.

"The police," the animal trainer explained.

As we hurried over to the balloon, more troubling thoughts struck me. A loose tiger and Sheriff Slim Colley sure didn't go together in my mind. And we'd just run from the field. I hadn't seen the sheriff about.

Near the balloon, I turned to question Rand Buchanan. But at once I spotted trouble. The men who'd chased us were headed our way, Brown Suit in the lead. The other man kept his head down, his face still hidden by his hat.

"Those men there," I said to the Great Buchanan, pointing. "They're the ones we overheard."

"Then you'd best hide. Climb into the gondola, that basket there. I'll see if I can send them away."

I nodded, though how could we hide? The men had seen us, surely. Besides, why would the Great Buchanan want to send the men away? Why not hold them and get some answers?

"Gal, I wanna give 'im a piece of my mind," Leo piped up, his hands balled into fists and his face red. I knew he meant the man he took to be his father.

"Not now," I said. With each step toward the gondola, I felt more and more uneasy. This whole set-up seemed strange. But Rand Buchanan—I could trust him, couldn't I?

"Get in quick," the animal trainer ordered when we got to the gondola. Leo and I climbed over the side of the square wicker basket. It creaked something fierce. We ducked down. Above us the red and blue gas balloon billowed out, all shimmery in the hot breeze. A heavy rope lay tangled on the floor. My feet got hung up in it as soon as I crouched low, but I kicked free. Peeking through a gap in the wicker, I watched the two men cross the field toward us.

"Stay down," Rand Buchanan instructed us. "And keep still." Then he stalked off to meet the two men.

As we hid, waiting and watching, I heard a crackling noise on the other side of the gondola. Someone coming? Or something? I thought of the tiger roaming free. Oh, dear.

I couldn't bear not knowing, so I leaned across the gondola and looked through another gap in the wicker.

Walter! Down on all fours, the boy crawled across the dry grass toward us. "Jessie," he hissed. "Jessie Land!"

Through the gap I whispered back, "Walter, get away."

"Psssst! Jessie, you an' Leo gotta get outta there."

"Go away," I murmured. "Those men mean trouble."

"I know," he answered, right on the other side of the basket now. "That's what I was tryin'—"

"Shhhhh," I warned him. I glanced back at Leo. He still peeked out the opposite side, watching the three men. His hands clenched the side of the basket.

I could hear Brown Suit say something. Then he lowered his voice and commenced whispering.

Suddenly Walter popped up. He leaned into the gondola and exclaimed, "It's him, the Great Buchanan. I heard him in the alley yesterday plannin' to steal the tiger."

What? Rand Buchanan in cahoots with the tiger thieves? The thought stunned me. At first I couldn't believe it. Another of Walter's lies? But what if it wasn't? I gathered my wits and realized we had to get away. Now. I leaped over the side of the gondola and hit the ground hard.

Leo called out, "Gal, gal! Help me! I'm stuck in this dadgummed rope."

I hopped up and looked into the basket. Leo was kicking his feet, trying to get untangled from the thick rope. I leaned way over the side, tugging here and there in hopes I could free him. All the while Walter kept yanking on my overalls, yelling, *"Hurry!* Let's get outta here!"

Out of the corner of my eye I caught sight of something. Rand Buchanan held an object that glinted in the light. He sawed furiously at one of the ropes anchoring the balloon. It hit me then. Walter was right! Buchanan was in on this plot. And now he aimed to set the balloon loose, with Leo still stuck inside!

I saw the other two men circling the balloon, creeping up on us. Walter kept screaming, "Hurry, Jessie! *Hurry!*"

I leaned in farther, yanking at the ropes around Leo's legs. I only seemed to be making a bigger jumble.

Then I felt an odd sensation. A little bump and jerk. Buchanan had cut another rope. Only one more held the balloon down!

I looked up to see the animal trainer dart over to the final rope and start sawing it.

Then I felt the balloon begin to rise. I clung to the side of the creaking gondola, hoping to pull it back down. Instead, I felt myself being lifted up higher. In a moment my feet kicked out at air! Something grabbed my legs and jerked hard. I hung on tight to the edge of the basket. Glancing down, I spied Walter clinging to me, trying to pull me back to the ground. Another jerk and Walter's grasp gave way. I heard my cousin scream as Brown Suit and Buchanan seized ahold of him. The balloon drifted up with me still clinging to the side.

Let go, Jessie, I told myself. *It's not that far down. You've got to help Walter.* But my hands wouldn't let go. They just hung on tighter as my heart hammered.

Silently, the balloon climbed higher and higher. I glanced down. Below, Buchanan stood watching. His bright white teeth gleamed an evil grin.

I shut my eyes as the balloon carried Leo and me away.

Chapter 13

Ker-blam, ker-blam, ker-blam! went my heart as I struggled to get a better hold on the edge of the gondola.

"Help me, Leo!" I shouted. My legs dangled in the air and my hands ached from clenching the basket so tight.

I glanced over my shoulder. Buchanan and the other two villains looked like bugs as they dragged Walter to a green flatbed truck. My cousin's scream for help was faint, distant. I couldn't help him. I couldn't even help myself.

Just when I felt I'd have to let go, Leo's face appeared above me. His eyes widened and his mouth dropped open. His dark face turned as white as my clenched knuckles.

"Hurry!" I whimpered as he reached down for me.

"Swing up, gal," he groaned, pulling on my arms.

It took three tries before I finally hooked my right foot over the basket's edge. Then Leo seized my leg and yanked. We tumbled together to the floor of the gondola.

For a second I just lay there. My mind raced. *I'm safe, I'm safe, thank You, God, for keeping me safe.* I gasped for air. Then I remembered my cousin.

"They got Walter," I told Leo. Springing to my feet, I gazed at the field below. I felt sorry and scared and helpless. I couldn't do anything for the boy now.

"Can you still see 'im?" Leo asked, not getting up.

I looked about. In a moment I spotted the green truck. *"There!"* I shouted. "It's moving now."

Leo got up beside me and took one quick look over the side. "The green one with the canvas-lookin' box in back?"

"Yes, that's it."

I watched the truck as long as I could till trees got in the way. It seemed to be moving toward. . . .

Wait. What had those men said? They planned to meet at an abandoned house east of town. Could it be the same abandoned house where I'd first seen the circus poster?

Then I remembered something else. Cami Starr had said that Rand Buchanan came to Santa Monica a few days ago to put up posters. Maybe he'd really been scouting a hideout when he tacked that poster on that house. I wouldn't put it past him. He might call himself an animal trainer, but I'd call him a common criminal.

"Oh, no," I whimpered. "Look what I've done."

Leo sank to the floor of the creaking gondola. His hands came up to rub his ghostly white face.

"What *have* you done?" he said, keeping his eyes shut.

"I let those men grab Walter. I—"

"I don't reckon you let 'em. What could you do against three men? And I'm sorry to say one of 'em was my pa."

I studied poor Leo. He looked sick from the elevation. Or maybe from knowing his long-lost father was a crook. I dropped beside him on the floor of the gondola and put my arm around his shoulders. "You still didn't get a good look at that man. Maybe he's not—"

"He's my pa awright," Leo said, holding his stomach. "I jest know it. I already tol' ya 'bout that hat of his."

"But, Leo, lots of men wear hats."

Leo shook his head. "Not like that one. Pa wore the same kind of wide-brimmed hat when he lit out. An' wore it the same way, low and at an angle. It's him awright."

I wanted to steer his mind away from thoughts of his pa. "Well, at least we're pretty sure where they're headed. East of town—to that old shack, remember?"

"Yeah, and us?" Leo said. "Where're we headed?"

Good question. I got to my feet and looked down.

I gasped.

"What, gal?" Leo started to climb to his feet, but I put my hand on his shoulder to hold him down.

"No, Leo, you don't want to see."

We'd climbed so high so quick it nearly took my breath away. The ground below looked like a patchwork of green and brown rectangles. Cars moved like tiny toys along the ribbons of roads. I spotted people gathered in a park and my stomach lurched. They looked like ants moving about.

Leo glanced up at me. His chalky white face had taken on a tinge of green. He asked, "You don't think they'll feed ol' Walter to the tiger, do ya, gal?"

Truth was, I had my thoughts fixed on Leo right then. He looked plenty sick. I thought back to last week when we'd taken an airplane ride from Santa Monica to Flagstaff, Arizona. Leo'd moaned most of the way there. And something about this balloon ride was worse. I felt kind of sick myself, what with the swinging of the creaking basket and the dips and rises as the wind took the balloon. Plus I couldn't stop worrying how we'd ever get down.

I didn't have an answer to any of it. How to help Leo. How to get us down.

Least of all, how to rescue my cousin.

Chapter 14

I leaned out of the creaking basket and studied the ground. Far below I spotted a road winding up a hill. Along it I saw a big, open green space and the roof of a large building in some trees. It seemed familiar. Then I spied tiny figures moving out onto the green field.

All at once I knew. It had to be....

"Leo!" I yelled. *"Look!"*

My friend sprang up from the floor and looked down. "What'd ya see, gal?"

"Will Rogers' ranch," I said, excited. "See that green part? It's the polo field! See the horses? And the people? And I'll bet Daddy's down there." Loud as I could, I yelled, *"Daddy! Daddy! Help us!"*

"They can't hear you," Leo groaned, plopping back down.

"Daddy!" I called again, though I knew Leo was right. Besides, even if Daddy did hear me, what could he do? No one could help us.

The balloon kept sailing. Looking left, I spied a bluish-gray color stretched out far as I could see. The ocean! From up here it looked so big. Like it went on forever. Like— Suddenly a horrible thought struck me. *What if we drift out over the water?*

I quickly put it out of my mind.

Then my eyes fixed on one of the ropes holding the gondola to the balloon. It looked old and ragged. Like one good tug would snap it in two. I recalled Cami Starr talking about how she needed to replace the ropes in the gas balloon. My eyes went from one frayed rope to another.

"Leo," I said, "we've gotta find a way to get down."

He stood up beside me and took one quick glance at the huge, empty expanse of blue. He swallowed—hard.

"Yeah, b-b-but how?" he said. His voice sounded shaky, and his face was still pale. He looked at me. "You know, gal, I could kick myself now, but I never did learn to swim."

Just then a gust of wind came in off the ocean. The balloon veered right, moving us farther inland.

"Whoa!" Leo moaned, holding his stomach.

"Well, at least we don't have to worry about swimming."

I tried to think of a way down, though my eyes kept straying to the frayed ropes. I knew I should tell Leo about our predicament. But I just couldn't. Instead, I tried to think harder. There must be some way to fly this contraption, to bring it down.

I noticed several sandbags hanging from the sides of the gondola. One lay leaking on the floor by my foot. I reached down and picked it up. It was heavy.

"What do you think these do?" I wondered out loud.

Leo shrugged, taking the bag. "Add weight I 'spect."

Suddenly I heard a creaking sound. The basket shuddered. I looked up just in time to see one of the frayed ropes unwind and snap. The gondola jerked and I lurched into Leo. We slammed against the side of the basket. The leaky sandbag flew out of Leo's hands and over the side. The balloon bounced higher.

"Whoa, gal!" cried Leo. "What happened?"

I pointed out the broken rope as we huddled in the basket. It now swung crooked below the balloon. My stomach grew uneasy with every sway of the gondola.

Leo gasped, "The rest o' them ropes look—"

He didn't finish his sentence. He didn't need to.

"We need more weight!" Leo exclaimed, panic growing on his face. "That one sandbag wasn't much, but now we're climbin' higher." His wild black hair whipped around in the wind, making him look even wilder.

"Collect yourself, Leo," I said, taking his arm. "We've just got to think. After all, folks wouldn't go up in these things if they couldn't get back down. Right?"

"I reckon," Leo muttered reluctantly.

I looked up and noticed another rope that went right up into the center of the balloon. Should I yank on it? I had to try something. I got up, held the side of the basket with one hand, and gave the rope a gentle tug. At once I heard hissing. I let up on the rope and the sound stopped.

Leo glanced at me. "Gal, what're ya doin'?"

I grinned. "That's it!"

He frowned. "What's it?"

"The way down," I told him. "Pulling this rope lets out gas. When the gas goes out, the balloon goes down."

I pulled on the rope again.

"You sure 'bout this?" Leo asked, his voice shaky.

"I'm sure," I said, trying to sound like I meant it. Mostly, though, I was just hopeful.

I pulled again. Gas hissed out, sounding like a basket full of angry rattlesnakes. But the balloon dropped lower. It worked!

I kept pulling on the rope. We kept going down, faster and faster. It spooked me some and I let up. Maybe it was best to go easy. We sure didn't want to crash.

After another tug, the balloon dropped lower.

"It's a-workin', gal. You was right." His suddenly cheerful voice didn't match his pale face.

I smiled at him and let up on the rope.

This time the hissing didn't stop. Gas kept leaking out. I jerked the rope.

Sssssssssssssssss! The sound kept coming.

"This can't be!" I exclaimed.

I looked at Leo. His dark eyes grew wide.

"The rope must be stuck," I gasped. The balloon kept dropping, faster and faster. I kept jerking the rope, but the hissing wouldn't stop.

I glanced over the edge of the gondola. A rocky cliff loomed straight ahead. *Oh, dear Lord, please not there.*

Down we went, picking up speed. The hissing rang in my ears. I looked up and saw the balloon start to collapse.

"Gal, we're headed for that cliff!" Leo shouted. "And if we hit it, this little straw basket's not gonna. . . . "

Again, he didn't finish his sentence. And again, he didn't need to. I knew exactly what he was thinking.

If we hit that cliff, we'd be done for!

Chapter 15

The awful hissing of the leaking balloon sounded a warning in my ears as the rocky cliff loomed closer.

Leo shouted, *"Look out!"* He threw his arms around me.

I shut my eyes and whispered a prayer the instant before we struck the cliff. *Dear God, please keep us in one piece!* A sudden jolt made Leo's arms fly loose. We pitched hard against something. I felt the basket shudder as it snagged and caught.

When I opened my eyes, I saw the hard, rough surface of the cliff in front of me. Up above, the balloon had snared itself on the top of the cliff. The terrible hissing continued. The gondola hung over the edge of the cliff and rocked from side to side like a flimsy porch swing.

Leo lay dazed at my feet. One of his legs stuck out through a hole punched in the basket.

"You OK?" I asked him.

"I reckon," he muttered, rubbing his head.

"We're snagged on this cliff," I told him.

He nodded. Then very slow and gentle like, he pulled his leg back through the hole. "Whoa!" he cried, peering through the leg-sized opening.

I looked down. All I could see were jagged, gray rocks

going down and down. There'd be no climbing out that way!

I looked up. The edge of the cliff stretched only a few feet above our heads.

"We've got to climb up," I said.

Leo shook his head, looking paler than ever.

"Leo, the balloon won't hang on this cliff forever," I pleaded. "If it slips loose, we're done for."

"No—no, we'll just drift down," he protested.

"Not when the gas's all gone," I pointed out. "We'll drop like that sandbag."

The sandbag gave me an idea. And it just might work if we acted fast enough.

"Quick, throw out the sandbags!" I yelled.

I stooped and plucked a leaking bag from the floor of the gondola. I tossed it out. Leo untied one from the edge of the basket and let it drop.

The balloon lifted slightly. We went after the rest of the bags, untying them all. I watched the last one fall and bust apart on the rocks below.

The basket crept higher up the side of the cliff. *Keep going*, I thought. *Higher! Higher!* But it stopped. We still hung a few feet below the top of the cliff.

Sssssssssssss. The hissing seemed louder. I knew the gas would soon be gone. Then, the basket would drop like a rock. We had to act fast.

I grabbed Leo's arm. "Follow me and don't look down," I commanded.

I leaned out of the gondola and grabbed hold of a rocky ledge. Clinging tight, I managed to pull myself over onto it. At once my heart commenced pounding.

Don't look down, Jessie Land, I whispered to myself as I eased myself up on the narrow ledge.

"Gal, I don't know what you're doin', but you'd better stop," Leo groaned.

My face mashed against the rock. I reached up and felt the top of the cliff. Yes! I pushed off from the ledge. My arms aching, I pulled myself higher. My shoes scraped the rock searching out footholds. Inch by inch I struggled up. Finally, I swung one leg up and over the top of the cliff. I drug myself up and collapsed on the rocky ground. Sweat streamed from my face as I lay and stared at the empty blue sky.

Thank You, God.

"Gal," Leo called out. "Gimme a hand, will ya?"

I rolled over on my stomach and saw my friend. One of his feet rested on the edge of the gondola, the other on the rocky ledge. The poor boy had his eyes shut tight.

"I'm here," I sang out. Stretching down, I reached for his groping fingers. Just as our hands touched, the gondola started to shake loose.

I grabbed his wrist and held tight. The basket slipped down farther. I pulled as hard as I could while he pushed off from the edge of the basket. His eyes flew open and I saw fear grip his face. I grabbed his other hand just as the gondola fell away. My friend dangled there, over the edge of the cliff.

"Gal," he gasped, struggling.

Give me strength, Lord, I prayed silently.

We stayed like that for what seemed like the longest time. Time enough for me to watch the balloon and gondola drop, banging against the side of the cliff as they fell. Time to see the wicker basket silently smash on the rocks below, exploding into hundreds of pieces. The colorful balloon lay on the rocks like a discarded scarf.

I looked at Leo. Biting his lip, he started swinging his legs, trying to get one over the edge. I pulled on his hands. Finally, he caught his heel on the top of the cliff and hoisted himself up.

We lay side by side, gasping for air. After a bit, Leo choked, "Don't think I—I ever wanna take up balloonin' agin."

While I tried to catch my breath, my mind whirled with images of the day's adventures. The furious scramble up the cliff. The frayed rope. The balloon taking off and sailing away. A tiger on the loose. My cousin grabbed by—

My cousin!

I sat up. "I nearly forgot Walter. We've still got to find him. And I think it's high time we get Mama and Daddy to help us."

Leo groaned and sat up beside me. "I'm as tuckered as an overrode horse, but we'd best git goin'."

Before we got to our feet I took one last look over the edge. I could make out just part of the writing on the balloon. **Death-defy.** I remembered that it had once said, **Death-defying thrill extravaganza.** It had been one death-defying thrill all right. And as we set out, I hoped no more such thrills lay in store for us.

By the time we made our way back to town, the sun
had slipped down in the sky. My stomach growled, telling
me it was past supper time. Leo and I raced onto the
porch and through the front door of our house.

A strange quiet greeted us.

"Where'd they go, gal?" Leo asked.

I shrugged and hurried into the kitchen. Empty. No
pots or dishes lay out. Nothing bubbled on the stove. No
wonderful smells of cooking like usual at this hour.
Square in the middle of our rickety kitchen table lay a
scrap of wrinkled paper. I went over and plucked it up.

Leo moved close and waited for me to read aloud the
note written in Mama's neat handwriting.

"Oh, no," I moaned.

"What is it?" Leo asked.

I read:

"Jessie and Leo and Walter,
Your daddy took off from the ranch early, and we took
Rudy up to Pasadena to see about a job with the U.S.
Government we heard about today. Jessie, for supper fix
sandwiches for yourself and the boys. There is milk in
the icebox and some apples in the pantry. Stay home.
We'll likely not be back home before dark.

Love, Mama"

"What's it mean, gal?" Leo wondered.

I turned to him, wadding the note in my fist. "It means
we'll have to find Walter without their help."

Chapter 16

Leo and I grabbed apples from the sack in the pantry and rushed out of the house. On the front porch we paused.

"What you reckon we oughta do first?" Leo asked before chomping into his apple.

In my mind I pictured Rand Buchanan, the man in the brown suit, and the other man carting Walter away. We were no match for the likes of those three.

"We need help," I said. "We'd best get the sheriff."

We set out. On the way to the sheriff's office, I started feeling plenty low. After all, Walter had been my responsibility. And menace or not, I'd let the poor boy fall into the clutches of some bad men.

I noticed something strange as we rushed along the streets of Santa Monica. Not a soul seemed to be about. Not even at the door to the soup kitchen, where you'd always find a line of hungry people at supper time.

"Where're all the folks?" I wondered aloud.

Leo scratched his head. "Don't know. Seems mighty peculiar."

We headed toward Main Street. Still, we saw no one. Every once in a while I'd glimpse a face in a window or spy a curtain move. But folks stayed hid away inside. We came up a side street only a block off Main and stopped. There in front of me I saw the sheriff's tiny office. A sign in the window read: *THE SHERIFF IS IN.*

Good, I thought. Sheriff Colley will surely help us find Walter. "Come on," I said, pulling Leo after me. We went up to the door of the office.

I turned the knob, but the door wouldn't budge. Locked. Strange. Did he forget to take down his sign?

I looked at Leo. He shrugged.

I knocked, not expecting an answer. But then I heard a sound inside. The scrape of a chair on a wooden floor. I tried peering in the window. I couldn't see a thing through the greasy glass pane except a ragged curtain and a dim light. I knocked again. This time I heard footsteps.

"Who's there?" the sheriff muttered through the closed door.

"It's me, Jessie Land," I said, "and my friend Leo Little Wolf. Please open the door."

"Can't do that," he replied.

"But why not?" I called back.

"I'm on the telephone. Official business."

I heard shuffling. I'd had dealings with the sheriff before, back when Daddy'd been wrongly accused of horse stealing. I knew the sheriff could be difficult. But I was determined to get help. I knocked again, harder. And this time I kicked the toe of my shoe sharp against the door.

Suddenly the ratty gray curtain jerked aside and the sheriff's round face appeared at the window. He wore a sour expression. The curtain swung back in place, and I heard the lock click. The door cracked open. Sheriff Colley stuck his head out. Crumbs of some sort dotted his chin, and I spied a purple stain on his shirt. But for once he wasn't chewing anything.

"What you want?" he demanded, his eyes darting beyond me. Before I could even answer, he tried to slam the door shut. But I leaned into it with all my strength.

"Sheriff, you've gotta help us," I pleaded.

"Git *back!*" he cried. "I don't want that wild—"

He gave the door a shove, but I'd managed to wedge my foot in the opening. Then he yanked open the door and, wagging his finger at us, began, "You two youngsters—"

I pulled Leo after me and we rushed inside. Sheriff Slim Colley slammed the door shut behind us. Grumbling, he bolted it and hurried over to his desk. As he picked up the telephone receiver, I noticed his hand shaking.

"You still there?" he said into the phone. "Listen, I t-t-told you th-there's a t-t-t-t-tiger on the loose. You need to send someone over here soon's you can."

Now if that didn't beat all. A law enforcement officer afraid of an escaped animal that was nowhere about. At least nowhere I could see.

He clanked the receiver back in its cradle and just stood there, rubbing his eyes with the heels of his hands and mumbling. I looked at the half-eaten sandwich and overturned cup on his desk. The spilled coffee had formed a brown pool, soaking the blotter and a stack of official-looking papers. Coffee still dripped over the edge, making a puddle on the floor.

The sheriff seemed lost in thought. I started talking anyway. "It's my cousin Walter. Some men at the circus grabbed him and carried him off. You've gotta help us."

Sheriff Colley looked up, startled. He shook his head. "Won't do it—no way—no how. I ain't goin' out there to git eaten by no wild-eyed tiger. 'Sides, I heard tell there's lions on the loose too. If you kids wanna stay in one piece, you'll head on home, sure as shootin'."

"They caught the lions," I told him. "And Leo and I didn't see the tiger anywhere about." I wanted to get his mind back on the subject. "Listen, Sheriff, my cousin—"

" 'Course you didn't see that tiger," the sheriff said, stepping to the window and peering out the smudged glass. "That's just the way with them wild jungle critters. Stay hid, then they *pounce!*"

He yelled out the last word. I jumped, knocking the dripping coffee cup to the floor.

"Sheriff, a boy's been taken against his will." I pleaded with him. "Kidnapped! You've *got* to help."

Suddenly he stared right at me, his eyes fierce. "You're right, girl, sure as shootin'. And I will help. Right after that escaped critter gits locked up and I hear for true that them lions was caught."

"But Walter—he's just a little kid," I argued. "He might get hurt."

"Way I see it, you got a tiger on the loose, someone's bound to get hurt," Sheriff Colley replied. "And I don't aim for it to be me. 'Sides, way I heard it, that cousin of yours's the one who let the tiger loose."

"That ain't true," protested Leo. "Man by the name of Rand Buchanan opened the cages."

"Mr. Buchanan, the animal trainer?" the sheriff asked in disbelief.

"That's right," I said. "They're probably hiding out at that abandoned house east of town. The old white one. Leastwise, that's where I think they went."

From his shirt pocket, the sheriff dug out a handful of tickets. Circus tickets. He tossed them on a dry corner of his desk. "Mr. Buchanan gave me passes for all three days. And some passes for food to boot. He's a gentleman, sure as shootin'. No wonder they call 'im the Great Buchanan."

I could scarce believe my ears. I said, "How could a grown man, and a sheriff no less, let himself be bribed by a couple of circus tickets and a handful of sweets?"

Sheriff Colley's face reddened. His head bobbed on his neck like it was about to come loose.

"*Out,* you two!" he ordered, pointing his plump finger at the door. "Git on out o' here and go home!"

"But—" I began.

"*Out!*"

"Ya gotta listen to us—" Leo pleaded.

But the sheriff wouldn't listen. He grabbed us by the sleeves and scooted us to the door. Then he undid the lock and opened the door just wide enough to push us through.

Then he slammed the door shut behind us. I heard the lock click. Leo and I stood on the sidewalk. I glanced down the street. Still not a soul in sight. Not one soul to help us find cousin Walter.

Chapter 17

"What now, gal?" Leo asked.

"We'll have to go after Walter ourselves," I said, determined.

He didn't ask how, and I couldn't have answered him. We just headed east. Toward the winding road outside town that led to the abandoned house.

When we reached the edge of town, the sky had begun to darken. I wished we'd had our bicycles, but they were back at the circus. We'd just have to hoof it.

The last building we came upon was an old, run-down garage. A faded tin sign read **Mac's Car and Truck Repairs.** A green car missing all four tires sat out front.

I heard voices coming from inside the shabby building. Someone said the word *tiger* and I stopped. I peeked in. The dark garage gave off the heavy smell of dirty oil and burned-up automobile parts. I saw shadowy shapes inside. They spoke with the hard voices of angry men.

"I heard it chased some kids down Main. Woulda killed 'em dead if Hal Stone hadn't thrown a bottle at it."

I figured "it" to mean Attila. I wondered if the story about the kids was true or just a rumor.

Someone else chimed in, "I heard tell some Okie kid

let that tiger loose."

The first man snarled, *"Okies!* Who needs 'em?"

"They're all thieves," grumbled another man. "My brother was loading soap at the warehouse, and this pair of Okies come by and made off with a box."

"What's an Okie gonna do with soap?" someone chuckled.

Everyone in the garage commenced laughing. I felt my face heat up. What nerve! I wanted to tell them off good.

But something stopped me. A clicking noise. I recognized it at once. I'd heard it before, back in Oklahoma, when Daddy had to protect the chickens from roving coyotes. It was the click of a rifle being cocked.

I spun around to Leo. "They're going to *shoot* the tiger!"

He nodded, frowning. "I reckon so, gal. We'd best skedaddle." He pulled me back from the doorway.

We raced away. When we slowed, I told my almost-brother, "Walter's in more trouble than we thought. Now there's these folks running around wanting to shoot up the place. We'd best hurry and find him."

As we hiked toward the old clapboard house where I'd first seen the circus poster, it hit me. I should've left Mama and Daddy some kind of note letting them know where we were headed. *Fool girl!*

Night came on quickly with no moon to soften the darkness. Leo and I stumbled down the dark, rutted road. We walked for what seemed like hours. My mind whirled with thoughts of trouble. The trouble Walter had brought on. The trouble I'd be in if we didn't get him out of this fix.

We trudged silently on. Then I thought I heard something. Music? It sounded like a tune played on a radio far away. It drifted to us on the warm breeze.

"You hear that?" I asked, stopping to listen close.

"Sure do," Leo replied. "Let's git goin'."

We commenced trotting along the pitch black road. Twice we both tripped and fell to our knees. But we scrambled back to our feet and hurried on.

Suddenly Leo stopped and exclaimed, "Hey, gal, lookit!"

I studied the darkness ahead. I couldn't see— Wait. There! The faint glow of a light. We hurried on.

Soon we came close to the old house. The peeling white paint on the clapboards gave off a faint glow. Light spilled from one large, broken window, making a yellow rectangle on the ground. The front door stood open, but I couldn't see inside. In the yard I noticed a dark shape. The flatbed truck! The very one that had carried Walter away.

"Come on," I whispered, creeping toward the house.

We crouched below the broken-out window. I heard a radio announcer say something about "the world's greatest oatmeal." Then a cowboy song started up. I inched up to peek through the window.

"Careful, gal," Leo whispered, staying low. "You're gonna git us caught."

"I'm not planning to make a racket," I whispered back.

I slipped up until I could just glimpse over the sill. I

spied two chairs and a table with a bottle of milk on it. Beyond that I made out a broken-down, tan couch with the stuffing spilling out. Lying on the couch was Walter!

I heard someone speak and then footsteps. I eased down below the sill and listened hard. A man's deep voice grumbled, "It's past dark. What's keepin' Eugene?"

Someone else grunted a reply I couldn't hear.

The first voice sounded like it belonged to one of the men we'd overheard at the circus. The man with the wide-brimmed hat, the man Leo took to be his pa.

"Who's in there?" murmured Leo, crouching beside me.

"Walter—and some men," I whispered.

"Who?" Leo asked, his voice no more than a breath. I figured he wondered if it was his pa inside.

I shrugged.

Just as I edged up to the window again, I heard a loud bump and the sound of the table being scooted on the wooden floor. Then Rand Buchanan's dark face leaned out the window, only inches from mine. His bright, mean smile scared the living daylights out of me. I lurched back.

"Ha, the kiddo!" Buchanan yelled. His arm shot out and grabbed my wrist.

"Awk!" I cried. "Leo, *help!*"

Buchanan grimaced as he reached out to try and grip me better. His angry eyes darted about.

At that moment I felt the sharp sting of Leo's rope on my hands. He had sprung to his feet and started slapping his coiled rope across the animal trainer's arm.

"Yeow!" Buchanan shouted, jerking his hand back and letting me loose. I leaped back. "Come back here, kiddo!"

Leo and I raced into the shadows and hid near the truck. Another man appeared in the window beside Buchanan. He wore a wide-brimmed brown hat pulled down low over his face. All I could see of him was his broad chin and tufts of black hair poking out beneath the hat.

"It's that red-headed girl and her little pal," Buchanan said, rubbing his forearm. "Go get them."

I didn't intend to get grabbed by the likes of them. Clutching Leo's hand, I raced to the other side of the truck. I glanced back and saw Leo's maybe-pa leap out the open window and start after us. But it wasn't his coming that stopped my heart.

"Jessie!" Walter wailed pitifully from inside the house. "Jessie, help me!" The poor boy sounded so scared it broke my heart. If only I could go back for him.

"Gal—" Leo began, but I covered his mouth.

I couldn't see the man, but I heard his footsteps. He seemed to be shuffling back and forth in the dark. Searching for us and no doubt all set to wring our necks.

"You see them?" Buchanan yelled.

The other man grunted a reply. I heard him stomp up on the porch and go back in.

Then it came again. Walter's pitiful cry. "Jessie, I wanna go home! Please, Jessie!" The boy's voice shook me. But how could we get Walter out of that house?

"Leo, we need a plan," I said.

"I could rope and hog-tie them varmints," he answered.

I considered it. "I think these varmints are too danger-ous. And too big."

Think, Jessie, I told myself. *There must be something we could—*

A deep, rattling sound interrupted my thoughts. What was that? It sounded familiar. I peeked into the back of the truck. A large, dark shape filled the flatbed. I touched it. Canvas. Canvas covering a—

Suddenly a low growl erupted from the back of the truck. I jumped back. *Gracious!*

"What was *that?*" Leo whispered.

I didn't need light to see. I felt hard metal bars under the canvas. A cage. With something inside it. Something alive and wild and deadly.

Attila!

"Git back, gal," Leo murmured, yanking on my arm. "They got themselves that tiger in there."

We stood back and stared at the dark canvas. I thought, *so they caught Attila after all. Buchanan and those men stole the tiger to sell to that other circus. Just like they had planned.*

"Come on," Leo whispered. "Let's clear outta here."

"Wait, Leo. I've got an idea."

"I hope it don't have nothin' to do with that tiger," my friend moaned.

I turned to him and asked, "How'd you know that?"

"*Ga-al!*"

"Quick, fetch me a stick." I told him, "Trust me."

I guess he did trust me because I heard him groping around in the dark.

"Hurry, Leo," I whispered.

Before long he trotted up and handed me a fat stick. "Whatcha gonna do with it?"

"Rattle the cage and get him upset some."

Leo let out a sigh. "I hope he's locked up good."

"Well, I *am* going to unlatch his cage first," I said.

"*What?*" Leo gasped. "Are you plumb loco?"

"Look, all we need to do is let him go."

"*Let him go!*" he cried.

I explained, "The tiger's all they really want. If the tiger gets away, they'll be too busy chasing after him to fret over Walter."

"I ain't too sure I like this plan," Leo said.

Plan? It was more hope than plan. But it was all I could come up with, what with Walter's crying and all.

I reached under the canvas and felt around for the latch, mindful to keep my hands on the outside of the bars. I knew to be careful, real careful. I intended to keep all my fingers.

When my hand settled on a metal bar I took to be the latch, I jerked it right and left. Nothing happened. I jerked up. It slid easily. I felt the bars of the door move free. Just a nudge from the tiger would open it.

I took a deep breath. "Here goes," I said. Then I commenced to banging the stick against the bars of the cage. The truck shook as the tiger leaped to his feet.

"*Grrrrrrrr!*"

A figure appeared at the lighted window.

"Kiddo, come over here," Buchanan called out.

I banged on the cage some more. "Say goodbye to your precious tiger!" I shouted back.

Leo moved close to my side. The tiger growled again, making a deep, rattly sound. Buchanan yelled, "You leave that stripe alone! You hear me? You get away from there!"

I glanced up to see Buchanan rush out the front door of the old house. I heard him come running toward the truck. There was no time left.

"Get out, you!" I screamed as I reached toward the cage to open the door. But before my hand even touched the bars, the door swung open, smashing into me. I sailed back and thudded to the ground, rolling over into some prickly weeds.

Owww!

"Gal?" Leo called out.

I didn't answer. I just scooted back in the weeds, trying to get far away from the tiger.

"Don't mess with that ca—" I heard Buchanan start to yell. Then I heard him run back toward the house.

The weeds rustled near me. My breath caught in my throat. The tiger? I didn't budge. My heart hammered and I tried not to scream. Then I heard a whispered voice.

"Gal?"

It was Leo crawling toward me in the weeds.

"Gal, where are ya?"

I reached for him and my hand touched his head.

"Ahhh!" he gasped, swatting at me.

"Leo, it's me!" I whispered, trying to dodge his arms in the dark. "Calm down, will you?"

"Gal, don't *never* do nothin' like that agin," Leo complained. "Where'd Buchanan hightail it off to?"

"The house," I said. "I reckon he didn't want to take a chance on running into Attila in the dark."

"Well, he's a might smarter than you and me, ain't he?"

Just then a noise came from the distance. I listened. It sounded like an automobile engine. I glimpsed yellow fingers of light poking through the blackness and bouncing along. A car! Headed our way!

My heart leaped. Could it be someone coming to rescue us? Maybe even Daddy and Mama?

"Quick, Leo, a *car!*" I cried. "Let's flag him down."

"Gal, I don't—"

I got up and ran toward the road. I stopped when the car's headlights flashed in my face, blinding me.

I waved my arms and stared into the fierce glare of the lights. At that moment it hit me. The car didn't sound like Daddy's old Essex. But the vehicle slowed, then bumped to a stop just a few feet in front of me. I ran to the driver's door. It swung open. I felt my heart hammering.

"Please help us," I pleaded, looking into the dark interior. "Some men have my cousin Walter in that house. And they tried to steal a tiger from the circus too."

"Tried?" the driver said with a nervous laugh. "Tried, you say?"

That voice. That laugh. I'd heard it before.

My eyes dropped to the ground. The man wore white shoes. No. White spats covering his shoes. A door slammed and I heard someone stomp about on the porch.

"Eugene, that you?" Buchanan shouted. "You're late."

Eugene. The man in the brown suit and the white spats. The one I'd heard plotting to sell Attila to that other circus. I spun around. But before I could run off the man grabbed my arm.

I peered into the darkness, looking for Leo, as Eugene dragged me toward the lighted porch. I didn't see my friend anywhere. But I did see Buchanan and the man in the hat waiting on the porch. Buchanan's nervous pacing told me I was in trouble. Big trouble.

I'd acted like a perfect fool and managed to get myself caught. Now Walter and I were in the exact same fix.

Chapter 18

Eugene dragged me up to the porch.

"I ought to take care of you good, kiddo," Buchanan railed at me, shaking his whip in my face.

I turned away, refusing to look at the likes of him.

"What's goin' on?" Eugene asked. He held me tight. I noticed the frayed cuffs on his brown suit. Glancing down, I saw the scuffed toes of his shoes and his dingy white spats.

Buchanan pointed at me. "This one let the tiger go," he said.

"What?"

Buchanan reached out and grabbed my shirt collar. He shoved me through the doorway and into the ramshackle house. The other man stood by the kitchen table taking a swig from the milk bottle. Not only was he a thief, he lacked manners too. The wide-brimmed brown hat still hid his face from my gaze. I wanted to ask him, "Scoundrel, are you really Leo's pa?" But I kept quiet. I glanced toward the couch. There Walter lay, staring at the floor and whimpering.

I heard Buchanan boast, "We'll find him at daybreak. Cats stay where they get fed. And we just fed him before she turned up."

"You'd better be right," Eugene said with a nervous laugh. "Uncle Bob's counting on that tiger for his show. The money's ready."

"I said he'll get his stripe and he will," Buchanan declared hotly.

"And them jobs," the other man muttered. "We want them jobs you promised."

"Yeah, yeah," grumbled Eugene.

Buchanan stepped over to me and gave me a shove. "Go keep little Walter company," he sneered. "And mind your Ps and Qs, understand?"

I went over and sat on the edge of the broken-down couch.

My cousin stirred. "Jessie?" he whimpered.

I leaned down, put my arm around him, and pulled him up beside me. "Shhh, Walter. It's all right."

"What about them?" I heard Eugene ask Buchanan as they sat at the kitchen table. He meant me and Walter. I couldn't make out the rest of their mumbling.

I stayed on the couch the longest time, trying to decide what to do. Should Walter and I just run outside? Probably not a good idea with that tiger still loose. And what about Leo? Where was he? I hoped he had the good sense to hide until sunup. To keep safe from Attila and these varmints.

Suddenly I felt really tired. I wanted to lay back and close my eyes. To rest just a bit.

As I leaned back, I heard something. It sounded like a vehicle pulling up to the house. The three men heard it too and jumped to their feet. I got up myself. Walter rose behind me.

"You sit down," Buchanan ordered, pointing at us.

I stayed put and watched Eugene go to the window and peer outside. The beam of a headlight shone right into the house, reaching the spot where I stood.

"Who is it?" Buchanan demanded.

"Dunno," Eugene mumbled.

Buchanan stomped over to Eugene. He spun him around, grabbed his lapels, and gave him a shake. "Who followed you out here?" he demanded.

"No one!" Eugene insisted. "I was careful."

"Not careful enough," Buchanan spat. He leaned out the window to have a look.

Holding Walter tight, I started to edge toward the door.

"Rand Buchanan, you and your tiger-thieving pals come out of there!" a woman's voice shouted. It sounded amplified, like through a megaphone. "I've got the law with me."

Cami Starr!

"That fool woman," Buchanan cursed, going to the door. "I'll take care of her." He swung toward me.

I stopped dead still.

"Get back on that couch," he snarled.

A common thief wasn't about to tell me what to do. I intended to go straight out that door. But Buchanan blocked my— Suddenly an idea hit me. It might work, seeing how he'd hightailed it back inside the house when he found out Attila had escaped.

Opening my eyes wide, I jerked my hand up and pointed out the door. I shrieked, *"The tiger! The tiger!"*

Buchanan leaped away from the door, scrambling backward as if he'd seen the creature himself. He tripped and fell onto the floor.

I darted for the door, yanking Walter after me. From the floor Buchanan lunged for my legs, trying to stop me. But I jumped past him and shot through the door.

"Hey!" the villain yelled.

"Miss Starr!" I sang out. "It's me, Jessie Land." The car lights shined right in my eyes, blinding me.

"Get back in here," Buchanan threatened.

I sprang off the porch and ran toward the headlights, still pulling Walter along.

"Gal!" I heard Leo yell. I smelled chewing gum as he came up to me.

"Are you all right?" I asked Leo's dark shape.

"Sure," he replied. "I spotted headlights up the road a piece after they grabbed you. But I didn't flag the car down till I saw who it was. Not like some folks I could name."

Ignoring his last remark, I turned to the circus owner. "Miss Starr, did Leo tell you Attila's loose?"

"He's *what?*" I heard a man's voice gasp. Then I noticed a design on the side of the vehicle. The seal of the county sheriff.

Sheriff Colley came up beside us. "I didn't think there'd be no tiger about," he said nervously.

"Hurry," Cami Starr told him. "That loose stripe's the only thing keeping those three criminals from running off."

"Gotta git outta here," I heard the sheriff mutter as his

bulky shape darted toward the house. He waved around something I took to be a pistol. "H-h-hands in the air, all of you," the sheriff ordered. "Out here on the porch. On the pronto."

Buchanan stood in the doorway. He glanced to the right and left. Did he plan to make a run for it? Then he stuck his hands up and stepped aside as the other two men came out. Sheriff Colley made quick, nervous gestures toward his car as Eugene and the other man started down the steps.

"How'd you know to come here?" I asked Cami Starr as she opened the back door of the sheriff's car.

"From you," she said, surprising me. She explained, "I went to see the sheriff. He said you mentioned something about the thieves hiding out at an abandoned house."

Suddenly I heard Sheriff Colley shout. I looked up and saw Buchanan leap from the porch and dash into the darkness.

"He's getting away!" I cried.

"Come back here!" the sheriff yelled, firing his gun in the air. *Pow! Pow!*

The sound of the shots didn't stop him. But erupting out of the blackness came the roar of the tiger. Buchanan halted. Slowly he backed up to the porch. I guessed he preferred jail to getting snatched in the night by Attila. Sheriff Colley hustled the three villains into the back seat of his car. Then he jumped in behind the wheel and slammed the door.

"I've got these bandits, sure as shootin'," he called out

the window. "Can you use one of those other vehicles?"

Before Cami Starr could answer, the sheriff tore out, dust and rock spewing from the tires.

"Listen up, kids," the circus owner said. "Get inside the house and stay there till I get Attila caged up. Don't come out till I tell you. Hear me?"

"But surely you can't go tiger hunting in the dark," I said. "Even Rand Buchanan wouldn't go out with that creature lurking about."

Cami Starr said, "Rand Buchanan? In a ring, armed with a whip and a chair and a loud exploding pistol, he might've kept a cat at bay. But beneath it all, he was terrified. And that's not the kind of fear you need. The kind that keeps you alive in this business. His fear came from hatred of these animals."

"So how will you catch the tiger?" I asked.

"I'll beat the bushes and see if I can get him out in the open."

She disappeared into the darkness. We headed toward the house. When we reached the porch steps, I had a peculiar feeling. Like I'd forgotten something. Then I realized Walter wasn't clinging to my shirt anymore. I spun around. My cousin had disappeared!

I ran back down the steps. "Leo, where'd Walter go?" I cried.

Leo stood in the doorway and scratched his head. "I dunno, gal. I thought you had 'im."

I heard rustling around the side of the house.

"Quick!" I yelled. "After him!"

"Gal—" Leo began, but I couldn't stop now.

We raced around the corner. "Walter, come back here!" I cried. Light from a window splashed onto the ground. I paused and listened hard. Where was that fool boy?

Tacked next to the window I noticed the circus poster. In the picture the tiger looked like a child's toy. Nothing like Attila with his jagged teeth and piercing yellow eyes.

I called out again, *"Walter!"*

At once he appeared before us, out of breath, his eyes wide. He was sticking his slingshot into his pocket.

"I could just brain you," I threatened, grabbing his arm. "What's gotten into—"

"But, but, I thought I heard—"

The rest of his words didn't come out. I saw his eyes grow wider as he stared past me.

Leo grabbed my arm. When the rattly, uneven breathing commenced behind us, his fingers dug in.

"Uh-oh," he said.

I didn't want to turn and look. But somehow I had to. My heart pounded and my mouth went dry. I turned and stared into the darkness.

A big shape glided into the rectangle of light. Something big, black, and orange. Light gleamed in the tiger's yellow eyes. His mouth opened wide to reveal those terrible, terrible teeth. Teeth like deadly razors.

The tiger roared. We pressed back into the rough wood wall of the house. Trying to make ourselves disappear.

Chapter 19

But we couldn't disappear. It was too late for that now. The tiger growled and stepped closer. We stood silent and frozen.

Then Walter let out a loud bawl. He commenced sobbing and shaking something fierce. I feared his crying would upset the beast. So, quickly I clamped my hand tight over his mouth. Still he made a considerable racket.

The tiger bared his teeth and growled again. Then he slipped closer, easy and smooth. With no effort at all. Almost like he floated on air.

I shut my eyes and struggled to remember the words to "Onward, Christian Soldiers." They wouldn't come. I peeked at Attila.

The critter had stopped. He swung his large head toward the brush. He seemed to be listening.

At that moment I heard Cami Starr call out, "Hey, you kids, where are you?"

I opened my mouth to answer, but my voice caught in my throat. Next, I heard the sound of boots stomping through weeds.

Cami Starr appeared beyond Attila. "Keep perfectly still," she warned. "Don't even breathe."

The tiger turned toward her and growled. The circus owner, though, didn't flinch. She reached toward the animal with a thick cane pole she clutched in both hands.

"Come on, boy," she said, her voice low and steady. She prodded him with the pole. "Over here, Attila."

The tiger eased away as she directed him with the pole. "Thattaboy," she said, urging him on.

When the critter had taken no more than four steps from us, I felt Walter move. He reached into his pocket. I knew at once what he was up to. The slingshot!

"Walter!" I shrieked. I grabbed the weapon from his hands. He fought me, and I felt the fork bend back and break. I wrenched the broken slingshot away from him and dropped the pieces to the ground.

Walter punched me and started crying again.

When I looked up, Cami Starr had led the tiger to the truck. I noticed an ease in her every gesture, in her speaking to the critter. If Attila tried to bat the pole away, she was patient. She kept after him. Then with only a couple more prods, she got him to jump into the cage. She latched the cage door shut and hurried over to us.

"You kids OK?" she asked.

"We're all right," I replied, even though Walter huddled on the ground, still whimpering.

She frowned at us. "Why didn't you go inside the house like I told you?"

I nodded toward Walter as if that explained everything. In a way, it did.

"You have a knack for comin' along in the nick o'

time," Leo remarked. He started chomping his gum with a fury.

In the light spilling from the window I saw Cami Starr's face relax. She smiled for the first time and looked almost girlish. Not like the troubled circus owner I'd known her to be.

She said, "Well, let's get you kids home. I hope you feel up to riding in a truck with a tiger."

I tugged Walter to his feet. As we headed toward the flatbed truck, I said quietly to Leo, "We can go visit your pa in jail tomorrow if you want."

"That wasn't my pa," he said flatly.

I stopped. "But I thought—"

Leo chomped his gum some. Then he said, "After you got caught by that Eugene, I snuck a peek through the window. An' I saw that man drinkin' milk from a bottle."

"So? I don't under—"

"Pa never drank milk," Leo explained. "Made him sicker'n a cowpoke with a belly full o' green apples. Then I saw him real good when Miss Starr and the sheriff pulled up. Wasn't him 'tall. I guess I just wanted it to be for a time."

"You two talking about that man with the wide-brimmed hat?" asked Miss Starr, pausing beside us. "That was Charlie Rivers. Used to work for Father a year or so ago. I guess Rand convinced him to join in this sorry plot. Along with that Eugene Miller."

"I can't believe all this happened just because Rand Buchanan wanted to sell your tiger to that other circus," I said as we headed for the truck.

"More to it than that," Cami Starr replied. "Miller Brothers promised Rand star billing if he got them some of my cats. Really, though, all this happened because of Rand's anger at me."

"*Anger?*" I asked.

"Anger that Col. Jack's upstart daughter came in and took over the whole show. I've been fighting that from everyone who works for me. But Rand—well, he had it in his mind that *he* should've been in charge."

As we reached the truck, I thought, *So that's why she never smiled. No one wanted her to run the circus.* I heard Attila growling in back, but the sound didn't bother me now that he was locked up good.

"Miss Starr, what'll happen to your circus now?" I asked the young woman.

"Oh, the show must go on!" she cried as she flung open the door of the truck. "We'll open here tomorrow. Then it's on to Monterey as planned. Things are settling down now. But tomorrow—tomorrow, you kids'll be my special guests. The three of you. And Jessie?"

"Yes, ma'am?"

"Call me Cami."

Chapter 20

When we told Mama and Daddy and Uncle Rudy about our adventures, their faces turned about as pale as Leo's had up in that gas balloon. They hugged us good. Somehow Walter got out of getting punished for all the mischief he'd caused. But that didn't surprise me none.

And as it turned out, it looked like Uncle Rudy had a good chance at that government job in Pasadena.

But getting rid of our house guests didn't trouble me much any more. I had my mind set on going to the circus. After all, we were to be Cami's special guests.

That next day was filled with excitement. The familiar smells of the circus seemed different somehow. The animals, the sawdust, the food, the tents. It all blended together to smell—well, just right. And the sounds seemed different too. Brighter and happier. Better somehow. Maybe it was that the circus had finally begun. Or that the animals were all safely locked in cages again. Or that Leo sat beside me chomping his gum, still my almost-brother. Or maybe just that we were guests, no longer working to pay for the things Walter broke.

Whatever it was, it was wonderful. We sat on the fixed-up bleachers eating steaming hot dogs and drinking down

large cups of cold lemonade. Cami even bought us each a
sack of sticky taffy and we chewed on that some, though
it gave my jaw a workout.

Then the circus acts got underway. We laughed at the
clowns squirting each other with water as they tried to
put out a fire one had started in a large doll house. I
gawked at a tall, thin man in a shiny green outfit who got
shot from a cannon. He looked like a green bean flying in
space and tumbling down safely into a net. The high wire
acts took my breath away and quickly became my favor-
ites. One man crossed a tightrope on a unicycle easy as
you please. Then a couple in dazzling red costumes sailed
through the air on the trapeze. Traps, Cami had called it.
They looked right at home up there, moving as graceful
as sparkling birds.

The animal acts went according to plan. Leastwise,
they looked like they did to me. Cami Starr herself came
out and went into a big cage to tame the tiger and the two
lions named Fred and Ginger. She looked at ease, just
like last night when she'd gotten Attila back in his cage.

She even introduced us to the large crowd.

"I want everyone in the audience to meet some youngsters who helped make this circus happen today," Cami
shouted through her megaphone. She wore a bright red
cape and swung a black cane in the air. The same cape
and cane her father had in the pictures of him hanging
outside the big top. "Santa Monica's own Jessie Land!
Leo Little Wolf! Walter Tyler! Will you kids please stand
up?"

We did and the people all clapped. It was kind of embarrassing, to tell the truth.

While everyone's eyes were on the grand finale taking place in the ring, I looked from my almost-brother Leo to my cousin Walter. Walter, who'd been the cause of so much trouble. He sure could make a pest of himself. Then I thought of how angry I'd been at him and Uncle Rudy the past few days. And how if you didn't watch out, anger could eat you up. Just like a tiger named Attila.

So how was I supposed to treat Walter now? I decided then and there that if Cami could overlook the boy's shortcomings, I guessed I could too.

Try to leastwise.

With the circus music roaring in my ears, I thought, *Jessie Land, why don't you just go ahead and be nice to him? Try right now. What's holding you back?*

I nudged my cousin and gave him a warm smile. Walter turned toward me, smirked, and stuck out his tongue.

Well, maybe some things would take longer than others. Like Walter turning civilized. I wouldn't let it bother me though. I just sat back and enjoyed the rest of the show.

Glossary of Circus Slang

big top: large tent for the main circus acts
bull: elephant
dog and pony show: scornful phrase for a small circus
grease joint: hamburger and hot dog stand
hammer gang: circus workers who drive tent stakes
horse feed: slim profits as a result of poor business
jack, kush, kale: money
joey: clown
Johnny Tin Plate: town sheriff or marshal
lotlice: insulting term for townspeople who hang around the circus
lot loafers: townspeople who watch the circus being set up
old man: circus owner
paper: circus posters
ring stock: horses, camels, zebras, and other uncaged animals
roustabouts: common circus workers
rubber man: person who sells balloons
stand: town where the circus plays
stripe: tiger
towners: townspeople
traps: trapeze